Reader Reviews of *Beyond t*

"a story of grief, regret, and the c
of forgiveness, second chai
An excellent reaa

"great storyline with engaging characters"

"the themes of forgiveness, second chances, and the power of love resonate long after turning the final page - overall, a beautifully crafted mystery romance novel that will keep readers engaged from beginning to end"

About the Author

Keith Williams is delighted to announce the release of his debut novel, **Beyond the Picture.**

Born in the English Lake District, he soon became fascinated by the idea of travel. Although never entirely achieving that goal, his career gave him the opportunity to visit numerous countries and it was as a result of meeting so many different people and cultures that spawned the idea of writing.

For a long time, his writing was generally confined to the world of business. However, it was the idea of putting down the opening words of an intriguing piece of fiction that really excited him. With the desire to turn his passion into a profession, Keith has written prolifically, resulting in the publication of this novel.

However, he is already exploring new themes, genres and ideas that he hopes will lead to further novels.

To find out more, visit Keith's website,

www.keithwilliamswrites.com

First published 2023
Copyright ©Keith Williams 2023

This novel is entirely a work of fiction.

All the names, characters, businesses,
places, events and incidents in this book are
either the product of the author's imagination
or used in a fictitious manner.

Any resemblance to actual persons, living or dead,
or actual events is purely coincidental.

All rights reserved.

No part of this book may be copied, distributed or
published in any form without permission from the author.

ISBN: 9781399962278

For my mother,

With much love and gratitude

Prologue

Rob watched the waves intently as they rose and fell, trying to lose himself in the grey sea's never-ending rhythm. He felt the tension in his body ease slightly, and for a few brief seconds, the guilt and confusion that had brought him to this place seemed to lessen a little.

And then, from somewhere in the distance, a dog barked, immediately pulling him back to reality, once again forcing him to relive the pain and anguish of the past few weeks.

Despite pulling up the collar of his jacket, his body shivered in the cool Autumn breeze coming off the sea. Although he was standing perilously close to the edge of the cliff, he eased himself forward to look down. Rob could see someone wearing a yellow jacket, possibly a woman, walking close to the shoreline. The dog ran ahead, chasing the gulls on the beach and towards the next bay.

Closing his eyes, he absorbed the coolness of the breeze on his face, willing it to drive away the thoughts filling his mind. But however hard he tried, the tension within did not abate. Unconsciously, he licked his lips, a salty taste immediately filling his mouth.

His discoveries over the past week had turned his life upside down. In despair, he tried hard to contemplate his future, but any thoughts stubbornly eluded him.

With the reddening sun sliding slowly behind the sea, he had been oblivious to the darkening sky that started to creep silently over him.

And then, out of nowhere, a moment of clarity. There was something he could do that was within his control.

He stepped closer to the cliff edge and looked down at the beach far below. It would only take one more step forward, and all would be resolved. He was drawn to the moving waves now crashing onto the pebbly beach. Faster and stronger in the rising wind, with splashes of white foam bursting into the air.

He looked straight down at the large rocks lining the base of the cliff, soon to be engulfed by the waves. Surely if anyone fell on them, they would be killed instantly? And what of the body? Would it ever be found?

Pushing these unwanted thoughts out of his mind, he took one of the photos from his pocket. She looked so happy, so beautiful. It brought a gentle smile to his face.

Closing his eyes, he raised his head, looking up at the darkening sky. Despite the coldness of the wind and the sound of the waves crashing below him, a strange sense of relief and calm now overcame him.

He knew what he needed to do.

And he needed to do it now.

Chapter 1

Rob

Saturday evening, 12TH September

Standing in front of the full-length mirror in the bedroom, he couldn't help wondering if all fifty-year-old men looked as old as he did. His short brown hair seemed to be turning grey at an alarming rate.

Wearing a white shirt and jeans, he was shocked to see the profile of his stomach had started to show beneath his shirt. Not surprising, he thought to himself. It had been weeks since he last went to the gym, and he couldn't remember when he last went jogging. *Maybe tomorrow*, he thought, knowing it wouldn't happen.

The more immediate challenge was that evening, another evening with Jeff, Claudia's boss, and Maggie, Jeff's self-centred wife. He had pleaded with Claudia not to go ahead with the dinner, but she had insisted.

So it would be the usual boring evening. Thinking about it just made him feel more depressed.

"Are you planning to stay upstairs all evening?" Claudia shouted from downstairs.

It briefly crossed his mind to say yes. "I'm on my way down," he shouted, doing his best to sound enthusiastic.

Reaching the bottom of the stairs, she was standing by the door to the kitchen. Wearing jeans and a red patterned top. She looked incredible with her long brunette hair tied back in a high ponytail.

As she approached him, the fragrance of roses from her perfume lingered in the air, bringing back evocative memories of their last date night, which now seemed so long ago.

At forty-seven, she looked much younger, benefiting from olive skin inherited from her Italian grandmother. Amy, their 22-year-old daughter, often bemoaned that she had inherited her skin tone from her dad. Now teaching English in Italy, they both missed her being around. Having come from a family with three siblings, Claudia had always wanted at least three children, but following complications with Amy's birth, the doctors told her she wouldn't be able to have any more. Although upset at the time, they knew they had one wonderful daughter and managed to put it behind them. On Amy's eighth birthday, she asked why she didn't have any brothers or sisters. Rob and Claudia looked at each other, reliving the anguish they had felt when they were first told. Claudia sat down next to Amy and did her best to explain it all to Amy. But as soon as she had finished, Claudia ran to the bedroom, eventually crying herself to sleep. Amy walked over to where Rob was sitting and sat down next to him.

"I'm sad, Daddy," she had said. "Are you?"

"Yes, my darling, I'm very, very sad."

As he spoke the words, he felt the tears rolling down his face. Since that day, it had never been mentioned again.

"You look amazing," he said, but the doorbell rang before he could say anything more.

"Oh god, they're early," she gasped, rushing back to the kitchen.

Still wondering if she had heard his compliment, he opened the front door, initiating the usual flow of pleasantries, and ushered them into the dining room.

Taking their usual positions around the table, even Rob was astounded at the sight before them.

Resplendent with a white table cloth, black slate placemats, and with each wine glass festooned with a black and white serviette, it occurred to him that even a maitre d' of a top Michelin-starred restaurant would be impressed.

And right in the centre of the table, a bright silver candle holder containing three long unlit white taper candles.

Now seated around the table, Jeff raised his glass, and Rob knew what was coming. This was such a tedious tradition.

Unashamedly overweight, totally bald, and with a penchant for bow ties, Jeff didn't fit the magazine editor's profile. Over a period of two years, Jeff had taken it from close to collapse to one of the country's leading magazines.

"It's so wonderful to be here again," he ventured in his usual booming voice. "Thank you," he paused briefly. "A toast to Claudia and Rob."

Formalities over, Rob relaxed in his seat.

Maybe this evening won't be too bad after all.

Claudia rushed in and out of the kitchen with plates of food. The fragrant smell of spices coming from the chilli teased their senses.

"So, how's your mum?" Jeff asked, just before he filled his mouth with food.

"Unfortunately, the dementia is getting worse," Rob replied. "Particularly after what happened to Dad."

"Really sorry to hear that," Jeff said sincerely. "So it must be about eighteen months since she moved into the nursing home?"

"Yes, when it became obvious, she needed 24/7 care. At the same time, we managed to find Dad a lovely apartment just a five-minute walk away."

Claudia continued to fuss around, checking everyone was happy. By now, Jeff was already on his third helping.

Maggie, who had already finished, cleared her throat. Rob dropped his head, focusing on the food on his plate. He knew what was coming.

"Do you know the last time we were all together, it was my fortieth," Maggie announced as if it was news.

Rob wanted to shut his ears as her shrill voice just grated on him.

"And now, our dear Rob is about to be fifty."

Obviously keen to change the subject away from his parents, insensitive as always. We obviously remember. We were there, you stupid woman.

But she hadn't finished. "I know the last twelve months have been tough on you both, and I hope you're now feeling a lot better."

In disbelief, Rob just stared at her. Shuffling uncomfortably in her seat, Claudia was trying to get his attention.

"Hope we're feeling better?" he started. "You do realise it was a bit more than a sprained ankle?"

"Oh, oh, yes, of course, I didn't mean—"

"Maggie, it's fine," Claudia interjected, glaring at Rob. "Isn't it?" she said pointedly.

"Yes, it's fine," he mumbled, even though it wasn't.

Turning around, he picked up a bottle of red and topped up his half-empty glass.

Maggie had talked incessantly for nearly two hours, dominating the evening. Switching between her three amazing children, their wonderful trip to Paris, and an even more wonderful trip to Venice. She described every single canal they had seen from a gondola in agonising detail.

If only she had fallen out of the gondola… Rob tried not to smile, with that image running through his head.

Now, on his second bottle of red, he was increasingly becoming more disconnected from the conversation. Looking across the table, his gaze rested on Claudia. Smiling and giggling at everything Jeff was saying. Annoyed that she seemed only to be focused on Jeff, he coughed to get her attention, but she ignored him.

"Are you okay, Rob?" Jeff asked, frowning at Rob's agitated state.

Ignoring Jeff, he picked up his glass to take another sip.

"Rob," Claudia snapped, the sound of her voice waking him from his reverie. "Jeff asked you a question."

"I'm fine," he replied dismissively. "It's just been a hell of a week."

Jeff nodded in response.

"Are we boring you?" Maggie asked, thinking it would lighten the mood.

If you would just shut up about your bloody holiday… Rob desperately wanted to say his thoughts out loud.

"As I've said, it's been a busy week," he replied curtly.

After a couple of moments of uneasy silence, Jeff cleared his throat.

"As always, Claudia," Jeff ventured. "It's been a wonderful evening." He paused momentarily. "But it's getting late, so I really think we should be heading home, but thank you."

Feeling embarrassed, Claudia glared at Rob, wanting him to say something. Relieved they were leaving at last, Rob chose to simply avoid her gaze.

Jeff and Maggie got up from the table and headed towards the hallway. Claudia followed immediately behind, unsure of what to say to them.

Gesturing to Rob to follow her, he managed, rather unsteadily, to get to his feet and made his way slowly to the hallway.

"Can I use your phone?" Jeff asked. "Probably best to get a taxi."

"Nonsense," Maggie protested. "It's only a couple of miles away. I've only had a couple of glasses."

"Um," Jeff said hesitatingly, glancing quickly at Rob. "I think—"

Rob was staring at Maggie in disbelief.

"Are you serious?" His voice grew in anger.

"The taxi won't be long," Claudia said anxiously.

But it was too late.

"It was your bloody drunken sister who killed my dad on his way home," he said angrily. "Your sister…" His voice got louder while pointing his finger at her face. "It clearly runs in the family."

"Oh god," she cried. "I'm so sorry, Rob. I wasn't thinking."

Rob realised she saw the anger on his face, and his eyes widened when she reached out to touch his arm.

"That's the problem," he sneered, pulling away from her. "You don't think. You damn well know you're over the limit, but you still thought you could drive, just like your sister. The next time you see her, tell her—"

"I've not seen her since it happened," she said, cutting him off.

"So what?" He hesitated, then shouted. "Thanks to your sister. I've not seen my dad either."

The truth of his words seemed to resonate throughout the house, resulting in a brief but uncomfortable silence.

"He's right," Jeff responded, now clearly eager to leave. "I'm going to phone for a taxi."

Leaning against the wall, Rob's gaze was fixed on Maggie.

"I'm so sorry," Maggie proffered, anguish all over her face. Her face was contorted as she wrung her hands in front of her.

"Just get out of here and leave us alone," he said.

Although he recognised he was overreacting, he couldn't help it. Needing to get away from the situation, he headed towards his study.

"Rob, where are you going?" she asked.

Ignoring her, he stumbled into his study, locking the door behind him.

Hearing the front door slam, he assumed Jeff and Maggie had headed to the main road to meet the taxi.

With clenched fists, Rob stumbled over to his desk, slamming them down on the ingrained leather top. Feeling overwhelmed, he fell backwards into the old leather chair that used to belong to his dad. His whole body was trembling.

"Please let me in," Claudia pleaded. "Unlock the door."

Blocking everything out, he heard her voice, but not her words. His thoughts were too deafening in his head.

Gradually, his breathing slowed, but the enormity of what had happened twelve months ago returned to haunt him yet again. Sitting silently, he could feel a single tear track down his cheek. Instinctively, he lifted his hand to wipe it away but changed his mind, allowing it to continue its journey to his jaw and then drop to his chest.

Then more followed. Each wave fell easier, following the same zigzagging route into oblivion.

Chapter 2

Claudia

Sunday morning 13th September

The wind buffeting the bedroom window stirred her gently.

Opening her eyes, she lay still for a moment, as if not moving would stop the concerns of the day from touching her. She'd tossed and turned most of the night, so she felt tired, but far too quickly, the events of the previous evening flooded her mind.

It had been a disaster.

"And it was all your fault. Why did you have to say anything?" Claudia muttered, looking over at Rob, still sleeping heavily. She was tempted to wake him, but coffee was her more immediate priority.

What had happened to them? What had happened to him? He had changed so much. Always so encouraging, always so positive. But now, often withdrawn and distant. She couldn't remember their last proper conversation.

She had tried to speak to him about her desire to leave the magazine. She wanted to fulfil her ambition of writing a book. It was a big decision, so she wanted his opinion, his advice. But when she tried, his only response was, it was up to her, before he walked away.

The doctor had told her to give him more time. It had been a major trauma. But nearly twelve months had passed, and he seemed to get worse. Looking at him sleeping, he was a stranger in her bed.

Although it was light outside, the bedside clock reminded her it was only 6.26 am. Unable to go back to sleep, she got up. Throwing on a loose top and jogging bottoms, she went downstairs.

Switching the coffee machine on, she went over to the kitchen window. Although it was only September, the weather had been wintry over the past week, but this morning was different. The sky had barely any clouds, with a few wispy white streaks to the north. At the far end of the garden, the trees had started to lose their leaves, yielding to the demands of the autumn season. But the sight of the sun glinting through the branches made it a magical sight.

She adored the house. Bordering each side of the property were high hedges and trees running from the road up past the side of the house to the back garden, dominated by a large magnolia tree. She liked to call it her tree, standing as it did, close to the window of her study.

Hearing the coffee machine beep, she poured herself a cup. She had barely taken a sip when her laptop pinged gently on the table in front of her.

As she pulled the laptop towards her, she saw an unread email. She took a sharp breath in when she saw the sender's name.

Cautiously, she opened it.

Claudia,

Maggie is so very sorry about last night. She is devastated. We both know it's been hard on Rob, so his reaction last night was understandable. I know it was Maggie's sister that caused the accident, and of course, she shouldn't have been driving, but it's not Maggie's fault. As she said last night, she hasn't spoken to her since. Please reassure him that we understand.

At the end of the email, Jeff concluded,

And if you ever need to talk, just call me. I am always here for you.

Unaware she had been holding her breath, she exhaled and relaxed.

It appeared they understood. But she knew Jeff. It was far more likely he was merely being magnanimous.

Taking another sip of coffee, she closed the laptop. As she did so, she heard movement upstairs. Rob was awake. She wanted to tell him calmly that he had made a fool of himself and was selfish.

Hearing him come down the stairs, she readied herself.

She heard him reach the bottom of the stairs as she finished her coffee.

"Hi," he said wearily, standing in the kitchen doorway.

She tried hard to suppress the anger and frustration she was feeling.

How would they ever move forward from this? Perhaps they will never be able to.

Chapter 3

Rob

Sunday Morning 13th September

He woke suddenly, his heart pounding like an alarm had gone off. Feeling disoriented, with a dull, throbbing pain inside his head, he swallowed hard, trying to calm himself.

As the window blinds were partially open, the morning brightness penetrated the room, offending his eyes and prompting him to close them again. In his personal darkness, his memory replayed the previous night's events, the ache in his head, an unwelcome backdrop. Although he could feel his heart beating normally, the tension within him remained.

Hearing Claudia downstairs brought him back to reality.

Perhaps I could stay here all day. But he dismissed his wistful thoughts.

"That stupid woman," he muttered, trying to get the image of Maggie out of his head.

Driven by the need for strong coffee, he slipped out of bed. After splashing cold water over his face, he put on the clothes discarded a few hours earlier and took a deep breath.

Walking down the stairs, the silence was noticeable. It was unusual for the radio to be off. But then maybe Claudia also had a hangover, although Rob couldn't recall her drinking that much.

Knowing he would face a barrage of questions, he readied himself. As he opened the kitchen door, his wife swung round to face him.

"Hi," he said rather lazily, belying his anxiety.

She looked at him expressionless, waiting for him to continue speaking. As he walked over to the coffee machine.

"I think I drank too much," he said.

"You think?" she asked sharply. "If only it was just that," she added, without waiting for him to respond.

"What are you talking about?" he replied, pouring his coffee.

"You know exactly what I'm talking about." Her tone was still biting.

"That's hardly my fault," he replied. "Are you saying Maggie was fit to drive the car? No," he said, answering his own question.

"Don't be stupid, of course not," she replied defensively. "But there was no need to be so nasty."

"Ha! You always defend her," he replied. "She only apologised because she had to."

"Rob." Her frustration grew. "She's sorry, but it was you who stormed off."

"I didn't storm off," he said, walking over to the table. "I just couldn't deal with it," he added as he pulled a stool out from under the table and sat down.

They both stared into their coffee mugs at opposite ends of the table.

"We can't go on like this," she replied, the anger being replaced by quiet desperation. "I really don't think you would behave like this if Amy were around." She added.

"Don't bring our daughter into this," he replied angrily. "It's nothing to do with her."

"But it's true," she replied. "You know she finishes her teaching contract in Milan soon. You also know she's planning to stay here, so she'll be around to see how her dad behaves."

"You just don't want to understand," he replied, shaking his head.

"So tell me."

Rob got up, refilled his coffee mug and then sat back down, not offering her a top-up.

"I was angry last night…" he hesitated. "It may be twelve months ago, but it feels like yesterday. Everyone just wants to forget, pretend it never happened, but it did."

Before she could reply, he added.

"That's what I feel most days," he continued, shuffling awkwardly on the stool. "And when she said what she did, it's like," he paused for a second. "I felt I was going through it all over again."

Rob could feel Claudia watching him closely.

Staring down at the floor, he struggled to find the right words, but no more came.

"Let's talk about it," she coaxed.

"Oh yes," Rob started, his voice low. "What you actually mean is, let's talk, but you never actually want to listen. You never do." His voice getting louder.

"Yes, I do," she protested.

"I asked you more than once to put off last night's dinner." His eyes were now fixed on her.

"You knew it was the twelve-month anniversary, but you still went ahead. So, you will understand that the last thing I want to do is talk about it."

During the silence between them, he walked over to the window. He gazed at the magnolia tree his dad had planted shortly after moving into the house many years ago.

"You just want me to forget all about it, and you're constantly telling me I need to deal with it," he said softly.

"What?" she exclaimed. "That's rubbish. I just can't believe I'm hearing all this crap," she replied angrily. "If you don't like it, you know where the door is."

Feeling angry and frustrated, she stormed off out of the kitchen. "Oh, by the way, Happy bloody birthday," she shouted, slamming the door behind her.

He continued to stare through the window, wishing she would try to understand how he felt.

Rob remembered the day they first met. Though they were both at the same university at the same time, they met off-campus at a local supermarket. He had just finished paying for his groceries at the checkout when the person behind him dropped their basket, scattering food items all over the floor. Rob rushed to help. Two days later, she bought him a drink in a nearby pub to thank him. After that, they were inseparable.

He sat down at the table, wondering how on earth they had reached this point.

She didn't seem to understand what he was going through. Yet, even after twelve months, it was impossible to act as if nothing had happened.

***

Looking at the clock, he saw it was time to see his mum. Grabbing his jacket, he went to the bottom of the stairs.

"I'm going to visit mum," he shouted.

He waited for a few seconds, but he headed outside when there was no reply.

The wind had picked up, and standing on the front step, he readily embraced the sensation of the coolness on his face. He had thrown his jacket over his right shoulder but gripped it to stop the wind from taking it.

Briefly, he closed his eyes, and the sight before him suddenly changed.

It was Sunday morning, on a bitter January day, the ground covered with a thick blanket of snow. His five-year-old legs struggled to walk through the snow. Making a snowball, he could feel the wetness and the cold seeping through his woollen gloves. He threw it at his sister, Mary, just missing her by inches, and they both laughed.

"Robert, Mary… time to come in.

Simultaneously, they turned to see Dad standing on the doorstep, smiling broadly, wearing his favourite heavy wool coat and his well-worn fedora. As a quiet, courteous man who rarely raised his voice, hearing him shout out made them react more quickly

"It's time to leave for church," he added.

Mary ran ahead of him, but the snow was deeper than he thought.

"I'm stuck, Dad," he shouted, starting to panic. "I can't move."

"Wait, Robert, I'm coming."

Moments later, he could feel his dad's firm hands grasp his waist, whisking him up into the air, the remnants of snow falling from his legs. Then, his dad carried him towards the front door. At that very moment, he remembered feeling safe and secure.

Feeling his jacket fall from his shoulder forced him to open his eyes. Then, brushing away the tears that trickled down his face, he went to his car.

Being in the drive overnight, it was spattered with leaves that had fallen from a nearby tree. After brushing the worst off, Rob slipped behind the wheel. He was about to start the car when he noticed Claudia watching him from the bedroom window. Tentatively, he waved, but she turned away.

He felt a small but palpable sense of relief as he drove away. He knew he wasn't coping, but he just needed more time.

But being alone meant the bad memories filled his head even more than usual. He tried to focus on other things, but they were always there, lurking in the recesses of his mind. They would never go away entirely.

And he couldn't discuss any of this with his mum. Dementia had taken its toll, and he felt a further sense of loss every time he saw her.

The conversation was always difficult with her, but with Mary there, it often felt easier. And she had promised to be there this morning.

Chapter 4

Rob

Sunday Morning - 13th September

Originally a 1920s country house, Sunshine Care Home looked like a hotel, possibly because it had been for many years. Surrounded by trees and extensive gardens, it was the obvious choice for his mum.

Rob recalled the first time he had taken her to see it. By then, two strokes had left her unable to walk. Dad struggled to look after her, even with a nurse going in daily. When diagnosed with early-stage dementia, a move to a nursing home became inevitable.

Dad would arrive just after breakfast every day, not leaving until late afternoon. Every day except Sunday, as shortly after his retirement, he had become a lay preacher, so he didn't get there until after lunch. On Sundays, Rob and Mary would typically visit in the morning.

Opening the front door, the distinctive, complex smells of such a place filled his nostrils. Not unpleasant, but oddly uncomfortable. A combination of disinfectant, food, urine and other bodily odours alongside the fragrant flowers and bowls of pot-pourri scattered in the entrance area and corridors.

A number of residents were sitting around, many in their wheelchairs, some aware of his arrival, many oblivious. An old man sat in his wheelchair by the window overlooking the front garden, quietly chatting to himself, wiping his wrinkled face with a tissue, perhaps wiping away an unseen tear. Catching his attention, Rob smiled at him, but he looked away, seemingly lost in a different place and time.

"Morning, Rob. How are you?" Brenda, one of the care home assistants, asked with a smile as she walked through the reception area. Full of comfy sofas and chairs, it was one of three lounge areas for both residents and visitors to sit and chat.

"I'm good, thanks. How's Mum?"

She stepped closer to him and put down a tray of medical equipment on a nearby table.

"To be honest, not great," she said with concern in her voice. "Yesterday, she was really engaging well with me and the others. But this morning, well, she just seems to be in a world of her own. I gather she didn't sleep well last night, so she could just be tired. Anyway, I thought you should know."

"Oh, okay. I'll see how I get on."

"See you later," she replied, picking up her tray and rushing off.

As he headed off down the corridor, he felt apprehensive. Over the past couple of weeks, he had seen a marked deterioration in his mum. And there was nothing he could do to help her.

Walking into the room, he saw her sitting in her chair by the window, looking out at the trees and the hills beyond. Seemingly lost in her own thoughts, he felt an acute sense of loss as dementia had slowly taken her, piece by piece. Every time he saw her, it seemed to be worse. He held his breath for a split second before she noticed his presence, wondering if she would recognise him.

Will I be her son? Or will I be a stranger to her?

"Oh, son, it's you," she said, smiling, her voice weak and fragile.

Her eyes were always bright, despite her frail body. Releasing his breath in delight, Rob leant forward to kiss her on the forehead. But she was already turning back towards the window.

Feeling disappointed, he sat down next to her. He placed his hand on hers, but she pulled away when she felt his touch.

"What are you doing?" she said anxiously. "Why are you touching me? Leave me alone."

"Mum, it's me, Rob. I was just going to hold your hand." As she turned to look at him, he saw the confusion in her eyes. "Mum?" he spoke gently, trying not to spook her.

"Do you remember what you sent me when I was at university?"

He waited patiently, hoping she would recall something buried away in her memory.

But she remained silent. The scene out of the window still held her focus.

He knew this was not unusual, it was just the illness, but it still hurt.

Wondering where Mary was, he checked his watch. She had promised she would be here by now.

She wasn't.

As he stood up to get a glass of water, his mum spoke.

"Food," she replied. "Every Thursday, I went to the…."

Seeing her struggle to recall the name. "Post Office," he said quietly. "You went to the Post Office."

"Yes, I did," she replied, wearing a contented smile.

"And I really loved getting them."

"You liked pork pies."

"Oh mum, yes I did," he replied excitedly. "They were my absolute favourite."

"Mum, do you remember—" He started, but as her eyes closed, he stopped.

Where was Mary? She should be here by now.

He sat back in his chair and waited for his mum to wake up.

A memory from his childhood popped into his head. He returned home from junior school, upset that the other kids had more friends than he had. At the time, his mum had been busy preparing the dinner, but she immediately stopped. She went over and sat next to him at the kitchen table. "It is not the number of friends you have that is important." She had told him. "It is the quality of those friends. So be a good friend to one person, and they will be a good friend to you."

She had been absolutely right.

Suddenly, the door opened, and a young nurse rushed in with a tray of tea. Placing it down next to him, she quickly checked his mum, smiled at him, and rushed away without saying anything.

Shortly after, his mum stirred.

"Mum," he asked softly. "Would you like a cup of tea?" Without looking at him, she nodded.

As he was pouring the tea. "Your father is such a handsome man," she announced proudly.

"Yes, he was," he replied.

"But I thought he might visit, but he still hasn't come."

Eager to change the subject. "What did you have for breakfast this morning?" he asked. "Did you have your favourite eggs?"

"They didn't give me breakfast this morning," she replied, annoyed. Then, before he had a chance to answer, she continued, "I thought he might visit me, but he must be busy."

Her face was etched with sadness.

"Mary will be here soon," he announced, hoping that would cheer her.

"Who?" she asked.

"Mary, my sister."

There was no response, and again, a sad confusion covered her face.

"Mum, are you okay?" he asked, desperately trying to reach her.

"I want to see him," she demanded. "Why doesn't he come to see me?" Her voice became more agitated. "When is he coming? When is he coming?"

Her once alert and agile mind had become blurred. Memories, once sharp and crystal clear, were now disappearing into a fog, being erased as if they had never happened at all. The disease was stealing everything she ever was, and he could do nothing about it.

"Mum," he said firmly, trying to get her attention.

"Dad died," he said, pausing to clear his throat. "Do you… Do You remember that?" His voice cracking with emotion. "That was a year ago, so he can't visit you."

He watched his mum closely, but her face showed no sign of understanding.

"Mum. Do you understand?" he pleaded.

But there was no response.

Rob felt drained.

I can't deal with this. Why isn't Mary here?

Eager to do something, he poured some more tea and sat down next to her. But inside, he felt an ache such that he had never felt before, his mind full of half-formed regrets and a sense of horrible sadness. So together, they sat in an uneasy silence for what seemed to be a long time.

And then she stirred. Yet again, her gaze returned to the window. After a couple of minutes, she said something so softly that he couldn't hear her.

"Mum, what did you say?"

"Son, your father's not dead," she whispered.

He sighed deeply. Knowing it was the illness affecting her, it was pointless trying to argue with her.

Maybe it was best she believed that.

But how he wished it was true.

Feeling exhausted. "Mum. I need to go soon. Mary will be coming to see you."

She stared at him but said nothing. He went over and kissed her gently on the cheek. As he did so, she lifted her arm as if she was trying to grab his wrist.

"Have you found the photograph yet?"

"What photograph?"

Not listening to him, she continued. "It's a great place," she said. "I used to walk for hours. So fascinating."

"What place are you talking about, mum?" he asked, confused about what she was saying.

"New York, of course," she replied as if he should know that.

"Yes, you and Dad went there after you were married, didn't you?"

He looked at her but wasn't sure she'd heard him.

Desperate to get his mum engaged in a conversation, he continued.

"Didn't Dad get asked to go there to open up a New York office for his work?"

She turned her head to look at him.

"We came back," she replied softly.

"I know, Mum," he replied gently. "I think you said once you were homesick? Do you remember living there?"

But it was too late. While Rob talked, his mum closed her eyes again. Assuming she had fallen asleep again, he decided to wait for her to wake up before he left. Noticing a magazine on a small table next to her bed, he picked it up and started to flick through its pages.

After a few minutes, he looked up and was surprised she was watching him intensely. She seemed different. The vacant expression now gone—at least for a few brief moments. She had eluded the horrible disease that had started to consume her.

"You must go there," she told him, her voice unbroken and clear. "You should go soon before…."

Pausing, she pressed her lips together, seemingly trying to find the right words. "Son, I need to tell you something about your dad."

"Mum, no," he said firmly. "No more, I've told you, he's gone. I know it's hard, but that's the truth, Mum."

"But—"

"No, mum." Interrupting her. "I don't want to hear any more about Dad."

He was desperately trying not to get upset in front of her. "Mum, I'm sorry, but I need to go."

He stood up and headed towards the door.

She turned back to the window, the disease now slowly reclaiming her.

"Mary will be here soon," he said as he left the room.

Closing the door, he headed towards the front entrance. He heard her speak, "But it's important." But didn't stay to quiz her.

"Where the hell is my sister?" he said out loud, walking back to the nursing home's front door.

Eager to return to his car's solitude, he walked quickly along the corridor towards the front door.

As he reached the driver's door, he saw Mary approaching.

Rob stood, glaring at her. "Where the hell have you been?" he snapped. His eyes were cold, and his mouth fixed in a thin line.

Mary's mouth fell open, "Has something bad happened?"

Rob said nothing and kept staring at her.

"Sorry," she stammered. "I just forgot the time."

"How can you bloody forget the time?" he asked angrily.

"I would have been here earlier, but the traffic was heavy near—" Pausing, she added. "The roads are busy."

"Huh, the roads were busy by the shopping centre. Right?"

"No, I mean yes," she replied hesitatingly.

"Not exactly a surprise. Of course, you need more clothes, standing there wearing designer shoes, an expensive leather jacket and everything else designer."

Visibly shaken by his outburst, she took a deep breath.

She clearly hadn't seen him this agitated. Only his wife got to see that side of him. However, he felt the need to tell his sister what he thought. "It's always down to me. Isn't it?"

Two nurses were standing nearby in his sight, undecided about whether they should intervene. Wisely, he thought, they decided not to.

"All I can say is that I'm really sorry," she said, dabbing her wet eyes with a tissue.

"Yea, sorry, until the next time."

"You know what?" she responded firmly. "You get more like dad every day, but not in a good way."

They both knew this wasn't true. Although their dad always wanted to take charge, he could never recall Dad losing his temper. Feeling awkward, he pushed past her, heading towards his car, the leaves crunching beneath his feet.

"Rob, we need to sort this out," she pleaded.

Ignoring her, he got into his car and slammed the door. He seemed to be arguing with everyone in his life, a life he felt was starting to fall apart around him, and he didn't know how to stop it.

Mary was still standing by the front door, visibly upset. Seeing her, he got back out of the car and went over to her.

"I'm sorry," he said and went over to hug her, but she pulled back.

"You were horrible," she said, wiping her eyes.

"I know. I felt so stressed when I came out. She keeps saying Dad's still alive."

"Sounds like the dementia is getting worse," she replied. "Anyway, I'm sorry for what I said."

"I'll let you go," he said, quickly hugging her.

As he walked away, he made a mental note to buy her a less offensive perfume for her birthday, even if her existing one did have a designer label.

Chapter 5

Rob

Sunday 13th September

As he drove away, he breathed deeply, trying to calm himself. He knew he shouldn't have lost his temper. Yes, his sister was late, but she was always late. He took another deep breath, hoping the tension within him would lessen. It didn't.

Looking down, he saw his hands on the steering wheel shaking slightly. Gripping the wheel harder seems to make little difference. He could feel his heart hammering away inside, half expecting it to erupt from his chest.

Why was this happening to him?

Reaching the main road, he headed towards the coast. As he drove, he felt the tension ease a little. Above him, large pillows of dark clouds gathered, and raindrops were starting to hit the windscreen.

As he neared the coast road, he caught a glimpse of a ship heading to a distant destination. How he yearned to be on it… away from there.

Then the rain suddenly became more intense. Turning the windscreen wipers up high seemed to make little difference. He started to panic, and a blast of noise filled the car, almost deafening him. To his horror, he was driving down the middle of the road. Panicking, he jerked the steering wheel to one side, narrowly missing a lorry travelling in the opposite direction. As he did so, he hit the brakes, but the car just went into a spin, his tyres squealed horribly.

The middle of the road, the middle of the road.

Where had he heard those words before?

Where? When?

The car was now partially off the road. An awful grating sound filled his head as the side of the car slid against a tall hedge, slowly bringing it to a stop.

He sat motionless, still maintaining a tight grip on the steering wheel. His breathing now rapid, came in short gasps.

As he turned the engine off, he swallowed hard, trying to get his breath.

And then he remembered.

The middle of the road. The words used by the Police to describe the accident.

Sighing deeply, he closed his eyes.

On his way home one evening, Rob's dad had decided to pop in to see Rob and Claudia.

They then argued over something ridiculous. Harsh words had been exchanged. In his mind, Rob saw his dad waving goodbye as he got into his car. It had been raining heavily, and he remembered Claudia telling his dad to drive carefully. Shortly after, his dad left, but Rob refused to say goodbye.

But his dad never made it home. And all because of Maggie's sister.

The memory of that terrible evening made his body lurch forward. His eyes shot open. He tried desperately to push the memory away, but the pain and guilt were too much.

He looked further up the road, and another horror visited him. This was where it had happened.

He could feel everything closing in on him. He struggled to

cope with it. Not wanting to look at the road now, he closed his eyes tightly, desperate to block out any more memories.

But his own mind, his imagination, had other plans for him.

Cruel plans.

He was sitting next to his dad as he navigated the bend in the road just twenty minutes after leaving the house. The road ahead should have been clear. But it wasn't. A car was driving down the middle of the road towards them, swerving from one side to the other. Just before impact, Rob could clearly see the face of the driver, but instead of Maggie's sister, it was Maggie herself heading towards them, towards his dad.

He screamed, bringing him forcibly back to reality. Shaking violently, with sweat running down his neck, he tried to get out of the car. He needed air, but he couldn't move, his body exhausted.

Struggling to determine what was real and what was his imagination, he focused on keeping his eyes open. Yet there was one image that would not go away. He felt it coming, he tried to push it away, but it came anyway.

It was his dad, lying in his coffin. When they had gone to the funeral home, he didn't want to see him, but Claudia had persuaded him he should. As soon as he saw him lying there, he rushed out of the room. How he wished he hadn't seen his dad like that. But the image remained etched in his memory.

But an even stronger memory—his dad waving goodbye as he got into his car on that fateful night. The night when Rob had argued with him. The night Rob had hurt him. The night his dad died.

Remorse and shame enveloped him. There was no escape. How he wished he could turn the clock back. How he longed to have the opportunity of taking back the words of criticism, to have spoken words of love instead.

But there was no way back. What he had done could never be undone. As a child, his dad often said to him… 'Rob, we all make mistakes, but how we try to fix them matters'.

But he couldn't fix this mistake. He couldn't fix what was happening to his mum or in his marriage? How could he fix that? His words were empty.

Everyone seemed to be wanting him to fix things. But how could he? He couldn't even fix things for himself.

He hung his head, feeling empty and lost.

He wished his dad was there to help him and tell him what to do. But he wasn't there.

The last few weeks had consumed him. He knew that. He knew his dad would want him to move on, but there was something he had to do first.

With the rain now passing, it was time to go home.

Chapter 6

Andrea

Sunday 13th September

Feeling hot and uncomfortable, she looked forward to returning to the apartment. Her dark brown hair was pulled back by a single green band she had bought at one of the stalls in Canal Street, not that it really matched her dark blue T-shirt. But she bought it anyway.

Walking into the apartment, she breathed a sigh of relief. Although it was late September, it felt more like July as it was so humid.

"Typical New York weather," she mumbled.

It was so different from her home town of San Francisco.

Her hair was damp, and she could feel her t-shirt clinging to her back. Turning on the air conditioning, she stood in front of the chilled air now flowing into the room. Closing her eyes and feeling the coolness on her skin, she tried to imagine the cool breeze coming off the Pacific ocean.

Not quite the same thing.

Pouring herself some water from the cooler, she sipped, enjoying the chill that ran down the inside of her throat. Sitting at the kitchen counter, she glanced at the clock above the door, wondering when he would return.

He'd gone to watch the New York Yankees but never even mentioned he had been planning to go. Instead, he just announced he was leaving and would be back around five.

All week, she had been looking forward to spending their Sunday together. Unfortunately, those plans were now shattered.

He gave her a cursory kiss and walked out.

She hadn't said anything, knowing it would end up in an argument.

She was just about to top up her glass when she heard his key in the door.

"Hi," she said sweetly, trying to disguise her disappointment. Then added. "Good game? Did they win?" Trying to sound enthusiastic.

"Hi. Yes, a good game," he replied flatly. "What have you been up to?"

"Not too much, just wandering around the stalls in Canal Street, grabbing a coffee and then coming back home."

"Sounds like great fun," he commented sarcastically.

"Oh," she said. "I also bought this, pointing to the hairband in her hair.

He quickly glanced over and looked away. "Very nice."

"Are you okay?" she asked softly, feeling something was wrong.

"Of course, I'm going to grab a shower," he replied dismissively.

"Oh, okay," she said as he headed towards the bathroom.

She was still sitting at the counter when he reappeared, hoping the shower had brightened his mood.

Now wearing different shorts, he was in the process of slipping on a white T-shirt.

Without acknowledging her, he went over to the sofa, sat, and picked up the TV remote.

She watched him, desperately trying to understand why he acted this way. She wanted to ask him what was wrong but didn't want to worsen it. So she stayed silent.

After a few minutes of uneasy silence, she felt the need to speak. "Shall we go out and get something to eat?" Desperately trying to lighten the mood. "It's my treat." She added.

"I'm not hungry," he replied, still flicking through the TV channels. "I've already eaten."

"Oh, okay," she replied, feeling deflated.

She was now dreading the evening ahead. Feeling hungry, she pulled out a green salad from the fridge, tipped it onto a plate and sat down at the counter to eat it.

"So what was the score?" she asked, hating the silence between them.

"What do you mean?" he replied, still gazing at the screen.

"The game, I asked you when you got back."

"No, you didn't," he replied sharply.

"Yes, I did," she said quietly.

"They won, okay?" his voice getting more impatient. "Does it really matter?"

"No, but I—"

"Will you just give it a rest?" he said, interrupting her.

She gasped at the aggression in his voice. With the only sound coming from the TV, she picked up her fork to eat her salad. According to the forecast, it promised to be a cooler day tomorrow, with lower—

She never heard what the forecaster was going to say next, as his voice drowned it out.

"Now you know how I felt yesterday," he said angrily, glaring over his shoulder at her.

"What?" she replied, now confused.

"You went to work yesterday even though it was a Saturday, and I was off all day." His voice now raised even more. "You didn't get back until well after lunch." He paused, then added. "All you think about is your work." Glaring at her, almost daring her to react.

"That's not true," she replied, trying to remain calm.

He had never behaved like this before. He seemed so full of anger.

"We've already discussed this," she said. "And the extra money will come in useful," she continued.

He got up from the sofa and took a step towards her, hands on his hips. His eyes were narrowed, fixed on her.

"That's a laugh," he shouted.

As he did, he took another step closer to her, grabbed both her arms and brought his face close to hers.

"We didn't discuss it, you told me," he responded. She could feel his saliva on her face but ignored it. "Anyway," he continued as he released her. "They are just taking advantage of you."

She took a step away from him and inhaled sharply.

"Jim," she said, trying to keep her voice steady. "This is my fourth temporary job in the last two years. I'm still looking for something permanent, but I need to have a job in the mean-time."

He stood glaring at her, seemingly ignoring her response.

She took the opportunity to move further away from him. He had never actually hit her before, although it seemed to come close a few times. More than once, he had held her arms in anger.

She could feel her eyes watering but wiped them away quickly.

Suddenly, he turned around and went to sit back down on the sofa. Leaning forward, he put his elbows on each knee and stared at the floor, seemingly deep in thought.

She watched him closely. As he seemed calmer now, she walked slowly over to sit next to him. Maybe if she just said sorry, he would be okay.

He jumped up quickly as she approached the sofa and turned to face her.

"You know what? We're finished." His voice was controlled, but his face flushed.

"You're free to work as many hours as you like and read as many of those stupid murder mystery books as you like."

He remained motionless, still glaring at her, his hands on his hips.

She couldn't move. It was like being punched in the stomach. Her head started to spin, so she reached out to hold on to the back of the sofa.

They had argued in the past, but he never said the relationship was over. However, everything that they had tried to build together was now shattered.

They had met in Central Park nearly two years ago and became inseparable. She had only been in New York for three weeks, but her accommodation was not what she was expecting. The pictures in the brochure showed a lovely, bright and spacious apartment with views over Central Park. Instead, it was dark and dismal, and the only view was of the seedy area of Times Square. So after a couple of weeks, Jim suggested she could move in with him as he had two bedrooms, and they could share the rent. It all made perfect sense.

Images of their time together flashed through her mind. But she pushed them away, determined he should not see how much he had hurt her.

"You bastard." The ferocity of her own voice surprised even her.

"Well, maybe I am," he replied. "But all you want is to get married so you can have kids."

"Don't be ridiculous. I'm 25," she answered angrily. "Yes, I would like kids at some point, but not yet. But I do want a career."

"Huh." Was his only response. He was just about to turn away when he stopped.

"I don't actually figure in this at all, do I? You're just using me."

"What? I really don't understand you," she responded, confused by his words.

She studied him closely, and it seemed some of the anger was dissolving.

"No, you don't," he replied emphatically. "Not at all."

"What do you mean by that?" She asked.

"It doesn't matter," he said. "Leave it."

"Tell me, what don't I understand about you," she replied anxiously. "Tell me."

"Don't you tell me what to do." His voice shook with anger. "Who do you think you are?"

He breathed in slowly, his fists clenched.

Throwing his arms in the air. "We're over. Do you hear me? You do what you like, but you'll need to move out."

"I've got nowhere to go," she replied, tears now streaming down her face.

"Not my problem," he said, heading towards the door. "I'm going to stay with a friend tonight."

He stormed out of the apartment, slamming the door behind him.

In shock, she watched as the door shut, shaking the room.

For a moment, she didn't move, still stunned by his words. Then, feeling the emotion rise within her, she ran into the bedroom.

She collapsed on the bed, and her heart broke.

Chapter 7

Rob

Sunday 13th September

As he was walking towards the front door steps, he tried desperately to push away any thoughts of what had just happened on the road. It was more important to put things right with Claudia.

Just as he reached the front door, it opened.

"Happy birthday, again," Claudia said teasingly.

Stepping forward, she kissed him gently on the lips.

"Thank you," he replied, feeling relieved.

"I'm sorry about this morning," she said. "It all sort of got out of control."

Claudia stopped speaking, her smile sliding off her face as she looked at him closely. "Are you okay? You look like you've seen a ghost."

"I'm fine. I got caught in the rain storm, and the car went into a bit of a skid," he replied trying not to make it sound overly dramatic.

"Oh my god," she replied. "Are you okay?" she asked, reaching for his hand. "Did you hit anything?"

"Just a hedge. It's all fine," he replied dismissively. "But I could do with a coffee." He continued and walked ahead of her towards the kitchen.

Reaching the kitchen, he turned round to face her.

"Listen, I'm sorry about last night," he said. "I do know I have to get over it." Pausing briefly, he looked away. "I was hoping we could talk this evening?"

"Ah, yes, of course," she replied, raising her eyebrows, "But I need to tell you about tonight," she replied gingerly.

"Dinos?" he ventured.

"Rob," she said plaintively. "I know Dino's is your favourite, but it's shabby. It's your birthday, for heaven's sake. We need to go somewhere nicer than that."

"Oh," he said, feeling slightly aggrieved. "But we've had some lovely evenings there, and it was also Dad's favourite place.

"I know, but I've booked Café de Paris in town," she blurted with a grin, trying to change the subject

Claudia seemed more excited at her venue choice than he would ever be. But she was happy, and he hadn't seen her happy very often over the last twelve months.

"Oh, okay," he replied, not that it was okay. He much preferred Dino's. "I guess it doesn't matter where we go, really."

"I'm sure you will enjoy it." She replied, touching his arm.

He kept rehearsing what he would say to her over dinner for the rest of the day. He needed her to understand his guilt about losing his dad, how much he missed him, and how painful it was to see dementia taking over his mum. After last night, it was now even more important than ever to talk it through. And he vowed to be totally honest and open with her.

***

"Are you ready?" he called from the hallway.

"I'm here," she announced, suddenly appearing at the top of

the stairs.

As soon as he saw her, his eyes widened. Dressed in a short black dress, smiling widely, her long dark hair cascading over her shoulders. She was stunning. Wearing high heels, she walked carefully down the stairs towards him.

"Wow, you look amazing," he said.

"Thank you," she replied with a smile, then kissed him on the cheek.

"Shall we go?" he asked, even though he was having second thoughts and ordering a takeaway delivery after seeing her in that dress.

The traffic was light, and in less than half an hour, they were at Café de Paris.

As they were walking from the car, Rob felt more relaxed for the first time in a long time.

"I'm really looking forward to this evening," he said warmly.

"So am I," she replied, taking his hand in hers.

Over the past few weeks, she kept telling him to put the past behind him. But it wasn't that easy. But today had been different. She seemed to want to understand. A quiet evening was just what he needed, what they both needed.

Glancing at her as she walked ahead of him into the restaurant, she seemed a little tense. He couldn't understand why.

The head waiter led them to a room off the main restaurant. He supposed this would be a smaller room and felt grateful to her as this would give them a better opportunity to talk.

Opening the door, he saw the room was in darkness. Suddenly, the lights came on, dazzling him momentarily. People were screaming and cheering.

"Surprise, surprise," Voices shouted out. "Happy Birthday."

He was stunned. This was the last thing he had expected, the last thing he needed.

An awkward smile crossed his face. A glass of champagne was thrust into his hand as he scanned the room.

Still embarrassed, he tried hard to look relaxed and happy. Looking around the room, his eyes, to his dismay, rested on Jeff and Maggie. If there were two people in the world, he would not wish to see, it would be them. He couldn't understand why Claudia had invited them. He tried to offer a smile, but it wouldn't come, so he simply nodded at Jeff by way of acknowledgment. Fortunately, Maggie was looking out the window.

In the middle of the room was a long dining table adorned with a white cloth. Above it, a large crystal chandelier spiralled down from the ceiling towards the centre of the table, sending a glittering silver light against the glossy white walls.

From behind, Mary tapped his shoulder.

"Isn't it an amazing room?" she said, kissing him on the cheek. "Happy birthday, Bro."

"I'm sorry, I…" Rob started to say.

"No need to say anything," Mary said, interrupting him. "But I better get back to Mum."

As Mary walked away, Claudia came to stand by him.

"Make an effort, please?" she whispered.

"Why are they here?" he asked, gesturing towards Jeff and Maggie.

"They're our friends," Claudia replied, frowning at him. "Anyway, I had already invited them before last night's fiasco."

"He's your boss, and she's his wife. If you didn't work at that magazine, would you still invite them?" he replies tersely, ignoring the inference in her tone.

"Don't be childish. Why don't you go and sit by your mum."

"Mum shouldn't even be here," he said. "It's way too much for her."

Ignoring him, Claudia walked away.

Feeling uncomfortable, he walked over to sit by his mum.

"Let's swap places for a while. I'll look after Mum," he said to his sister.

"Are you sure?" Mary asked, sounding relieved.

With everyone seated, the room buzzed with chatter. Waiters rushed around with their note pads, hurriedly taking orders.

Glancing at his mum, he could see she was getting more and more confused.

"It's my birthday party," he told her. "I'm fifty."

In a brief moment of apparent clarity. "It's a shame your dad couldn't be here," she said in a whisper.

"I know," he replied.

Looking across the table, he noticed Claudia go and sit next to Jeff. It annoyed him that she seemed to be giggling at whatever he was saying.

The waiters returned with a sense of urgency, with two or three plates balanced skilfully on their arms. Moments later, they were ready to eat.

"Isn't this wonderful?" Jeff boomed loudly as he pushed his chair back.

Oh, no.

"A toast to the birthday boy," Jeff declared.

Everyone raised their glasses.

"Happy Birthday," everyone responded in unison.

Forcing a smile, Rob nodded in acknowledgment. But Jeff hadn't finished.

"And a big thank you to the very gorgeous Claudia, who has arranged this wonderful evening for us all. Rob is a very lucky man."

The smile fell away from Rob's face as he watched Claudia look up admiringly at Jeff. Then, as Jeff went to sit down, he kissed Claudia affectionately on the cheek, causing her to blush visibly.

Rob struggled to control his reactions.

So this was why Claudia dressed up so attractively. It was all intended for Jeff.

"I don't want it." His mum mumbled as a waiter put a plate of food in front of her. "Where's your Dad? He should be here."

"Mum, you know Dad can't come. I keep telling you that. Please, you have to eat," he pleaded.

Rob looked down the table, noticing Mary laughing and joking with the others.

"Well, at least she's having a good time," he muttered to himself.

"Where's your Dad?" she asked again.

"Mum, will you please stop asking about Dad," he replied. "He's not coming."

His mum turned slowly, looking directly into his face. Her expression held such a sadness that it almost broke him.

Feeling frustrated, he stood up. "I'm taking Mum home. She's exhausted."

He looked across at Claudia who was now glaring at him.

"I can take her back. I brought her," Mary offered as she came around the table towards him.

"No, I'll take her," he said firmly.

"I'm sorry, Rob," Mary replied.

Rob was unsure what she was apologising for.

"Come on, Mum, time to go home," he said gently, ignoring Mary.

Struggling to stand up, his mum blurted, "Have you found the photograph yet? I keep asking, but you won't tell me."

Mary overheard the question.

"What photograph is that, Mum?" she asked.

"Leave it," Rob whispered, sighing heavily. "Don't encourage her."

But their mum continued.

"The photograph of me, of course. The one in New York. It's my favourite one."

"Really?" Mary responded. "I don't think I have ever seen that one. Have we seen it before?"

"No, no. I couldn't let your father see it."

"Why not?"

Their mum went silent.

Mary looked at Rob, thinking he might know more. But, shrugging his shoulders, he helped his mum into the wheelchair and headed for the exit.

I just wish she would stop going on about this photo. It was ridiculous.

Walking towards the car, he felt relieved to be outside.

Claudia would no doubt be angry with him. But he was angry with her. The whole evening was a charade, and she couldn't have flirted more with Jeff if she had tried. He really thought she would try to understand him and help him through. But he was wrong. He was still on his own.

After dropping his Mum back at the nursing home, he headed home, confident Mary would take Claudia home. Noticing it was only 10 o'clock on the dashboard clock, he guessed Claudia would probably still be partying, particularly if Jeff was still around.

Pulling into the driveway, he couldn't see any lights on, so he knew he was right.

Entering the house, he decided to wait for Claudia to return. She would no doubt be furious and wouldn't want to wait until the morning to tell him that. So he might as well get ready. And a glass of brandy was the necessary first step.

As he was pouring his drink, his eyes fell upon the framed photos lined up on the sideboard. Two photos were of his mum and dad.

Why does she think there is a photo of her? Is there one? And if so, where the hell is it?

Sipping his brandy, the evening kept replaying in his head. But the constant questioning from his mum was unsettling him now.

He had helped his mum sort out her possessions before moving into the nursing home and…

"Yes, of course," he chirped loudly and nearly dropped his glass.

His mum wanted some boxes and old suitcases to keep in the loft. He remembered she had stressed they should not be thrown away. He had to promise never to do that.

But that was years ago now. So if, and it was a big if, there were photos to be found, they would be in those boxes.

Surely?

Within minutes, he was scrambling into the loft, scraping his knee in the process. Feeling an odd sense of anticipation, he scanned the loft with a torch. In the far corner were a few small boxes and a couple of old suitcases, all stacked neatly.

One by one, he opened the boxes, and each time, he felt a tinge of disappointment. Two were full of records, the old ten-inch vinyl that must have belonged to his dad, and another box full of ornaments. The suitcases were full of clothes.

Perhaps this was a waste of time. Claudia would know I'm crazy if she came back now.

Pulling the last box closer to him, he lifted the lid. A broad smile came to his face, recalling how he sat on the floor on Christmas Day. How he had carefully lifted each piece out of the box. It was probably broken now, but he remembered holding his train set in his hands as if it was made of delicate glass. His dad had helped him put it all together, and they both spent hours playing with it. A time he had felt really close to him.

He tried to push the painful memory away. But the damage had been done.

But there was no photograph. Rob was angry with himself for even thinking it existed. His mum had simply been confused.

Just as he was putting the train set back into the box, he noticed the bottom of the box was covered with newspaper. Lifting up the paper, he found a large brown envelope sealed with tape. As he pulled it out, he could feel there was something inside. So he tore off the tape and tipped the contents onto the loft floorboards.

A photograph slid out, landing face down in the dust.

Tentatively, he turned it over. He felt his mouth fall open, his eyes wide-eyed, now transfixed, lost in emotion. He could feel the hairs on the back of his neck stand up.

"I don't believe it," he mumbled slowly to himself. "I just don't believe it."

She was right. Mum was right.

The photograph was badly discoloured, but his mum's face glowed with an intensity he had never seen before. She was sitting by herself on a high-back chair, looking directly at the camera. Her eyes seemed to shine out from the photograph. And despite her serious expression, he sensed there was a happiness within her.

So much happiness, it made him smile.

Swallowing hard, trying to keep the tears away, he knew something else. She wanted him to find it.

Flipping the photo over, he noticed a small ink stamp with the name *Elliot Grossman, Photographer*, together with the address of the studio. He picked up the envelope to check if there are any other photos, maybe of his dad, but there were none.

Just as he slipped the photo back into the envelope, he could hear a car outside.

Knowing it would be Claudia, he prepared himself for the encounter.

With the envelope in his hand, he jumped down from the loft and headed down the stairs. Halfway down, the front door opened, and Claudia stumbled in, immediately followed by Mary, who was trying to keep her steady.

"You selfish bastard," his wife shouted, slurring her words.

Stunned by her outburst, he stayed silent.

"Leave this to me," Mary said firmly.

"Probably a good idea," he replied nervously.

"Yes, do," Claudia mumbled.

"Not now," Mary told her. "Let's just get you to bed."

He went over to help Mary, but Claudia pulled away sharply.

"Get off me."

"I'll get her to bed," Mary said. "You best stay down here."

After some effort, his sister managed to get Claudia up the stairs and into bed.

Sitting in the kitchen, he gazed at the photo, now lying face up on the table.

"Well, not the best birthday party I have ever been to," Mary announced, walking into the kitchen.

"Is she okay?" he asked

"You mean apart from being so drunk she can barely walk, that she had a row with her friend Maggie, I've no idea what about, so don't ask me, and the fact she is absolutely furious with you. Yes," Mary replied sarcastically. "She's absolutely fine."

Mary took a long breath in and aimed her gaze at Rob. "So tell me, my dear brother. Why did you walk out of your own party under the pretext of taking Mum home?"

Rob was opening his mouth to reply when he was cut off.

"Actually," she continued, "I probably don't want to know the answer, but you certainly have stuff to sort out with your wife."

Feeling it would be better not to get involved in any discussion, he stayed silent.

Instead, he pushed the photo across the table towards her.

"What's that? Oh, that looks a bit like… oh my god, it is… it's Mum," Mary said, staring at it.

"It's the photo Mum was going on about. I found it in the loft just a few minutes before you arrived," he said.

Turning the photo over, she said, "New York?"

"Looks like," he answered.

"She looks…."

"Happy?" he said, interrupting her.

"Yes, very, but I thought they had a miserable time there," Mary said, tracing the image with her fingertips.

"I know. They always said it was a bad experience. But Mum has not stopped talking about this photo for a while now, always asking if I had found it. I just didn't think it existed."

"Wow," Mary replied, still reeling from the shock.

"So what are you going to do about it?" she asks.

"What do you mean?"

"Don't you think it's a little odd?"

"When I was with her earlier, she was rambling, saying New York was a wonderful place. I just thought it was dementia talking."

He paused for a moment.

"Maybe I should try to phone the photographer who took the pictures. Maybe there are some others. Perhaps with Dad in them?"

"Are you serious?" she replied. "This is over fifty years ago."

"Mmm, good point," he said. "But it's worth a shot."

"Listen, I need to go, but good luck with Claudia. I think you'll need it."

"Yea, you're probably right." Pausing for a second. "And thank you."

As she headed for the door, she turned and smiled. "Call me," she said.

Chapter 8

Sally

Sunday 13th September

Wearing a blue floral dress and a silk scarf wrapped around her neck, she noticed a young woman sitting on a bench in the middle of Washington Square. She smoothed her greying hair and straightened her jacket. She knew when someone needed a stranger to talk to. She may have wrinkles on her face betraying her advanced years, but she was wise enough to know when someone needed to talk.

Changing direction, she walked towards her, each step agonisingly slow.

"My dear, are you okay? Why are you crying?" Sally asked slowly and deliberately, with concern in her voice.

The young woman jerked her head up, her eyes still damp with tears.

Shuffling closer, she leant forward, rummaged in her handbag, and handed her a tissue.

"Thank you," she said, her voice thick with emotion.

As she wiped her eyes, she studied Sally more closely.

Sally hoped her kind, gentle smile told the young girl she was friend, not foe.

"My dear, are you okay?" she asked again.

"I'm okay. It's nothing, really," she replied.

"May I sit next to you?" Sally asked. "My legs are quite feeble these days."

"Of course."

Loosening her scarf, she eased herself down on the bench.

"When anyone says it's nothing," she started. "That probably means it's something, but my dear, I'm sorry to pry. I was just concerned for you."

"Thank you, but I'm okay," she replied a little dismissively.

Sitting together in an easy, natural silence, they were two strangers simply sharing a park bench.

A young couple walked slowly down the path towards them. Their hands intertwined, their bodies moving as one. Every few steps, he kissed her cheek, and she buried her head into his shoulder. They exuded happiness, contentment, and most of all, love.

As they were passing, the young woman cleared her throat, breaking the silence.

"I had a terrible argument with my boyfriend earlier," she said, her voice heavy with emotion. "He was so angry. After he left, I just had to get out, and I ended up here."

Pausing briefly, she added. "It was really bad. At one point, I thought he was going to…" she stopped herself. She covered her face with her hands.

"What did you think, my dear?" Sally asked softly.

"Nothing," she mumbled, seemingly embarrassed.

"Did you think he was going to hurt you?"

The young woman's body jolted.

"No, of course not," she replied angrily.

But tears started to roll down her cheeks, revealing the truth.

"Sorry, my dear, my mistake," Sally said quietly.

The young woman pulled her knees up, burying her face in her hands.

The lady stayed quiet. She had her own silent tears.

A few minutes passed. "May I ask your name?" Sally asked.

"Andrea," she said, wiping her eyes.

"Andrea," she said as she placed her hand on Andrea's. "Just remember one thing. Always listen to what your heart is telling you but don't ignore what your head is telling you."

"I'm Sally, by the way. I can't stay long as my husband is not too well and will be wondering where I am," she said. "But I do hate seeing you so upset."

"You've been really kind," Andrea replied. "And I'm sorry I was rude."

"My dear, I never thought you were rude. You were hurting."

Sally let go of Andrea's hand and started to get to her feet.

"Can I ask you something?" Andrea asked.

"Certainly. What is it?"

"You mentioned your husband. Can I ask how long you've been married?"

Sally laughed softly. "Do you mind if I sit down again?"

"Of course," Andrea replied. "But your husband…?"

"It's okay, my dear. Allow me to answer your question, but it's not a short answer."

Sally placed her bag on the bench next to her and took Andrea's hand again.

"I met him fifty-six years ago tomorrow. But, I have to admit I was still married at the time." Sally paused for a moment. "I had only been married to my first husband for less than a year... when he first hit me."

Andrea gasped, covering her mouth with her hand.

"It wasn't the last time. It was quite a few times," Sally added.

"I'm so sorry," Andrea said.

"But one day, I came home late from work. He had been drinking, and I ended up with a broken nose."

Andrea turned to face Sally, squeezing her frail hand. "What did you do?"

"I ran out of the apartment, and do you know where I went?" she asked.

Andrea shook her head.

"Here," she continued, pointing her finger downwards. "This very same bench."

Sally looked into the distance for a few seconds, seemingly lost in her thoughts.

"I felt so hurt. I even felt guilty, thinking that perhaps it was all my fault. That I wasn't a good enough wife," she said as she wiped her eyes with a tissue. "I just couldn't stop crying." She paused again as she got a little breathless. "And then, this old lady came and sat next to me... I didn't notice her at first... I was too busy feeling sorry for myself. She put her hand on mine, and I poured out my heart to her."

Again, Sally looked away into the distance as if reliving that moment many years ago. "She sat next to me for a while. She didn't say anything. She just held my hand," Sally continued. "And then she spoke the words that I used earlier. Always listen to your heart but don't ignore what your head is telling you."

"So what did you do?" Andrea asked.

"I went back to the apartment, not far from here but not where we live now." She paused again, her voice now sounding a little weaker. "I just packed a bag and walked out. I didn't take anything else, and I never went back."

"So, when did you meet your new husband? Sorry, what's his name?"

"Larry," she replied. "It was only about three weeks later. I was trying to hail a cab outside Central Station. The street was really busy, and it was raining."

Sally stopped briefly as she recalled the scene.

"A cab eventually stopped, and I went to jump in, but it was actually stopping to pick up somebody else. This handsome man got in the cab before I reached it, but he offered to share the ride when he saw me. Since then, we have shared our entire lives together."

"That's amazing," Andrea replied.

"Yes, it was. I knew I loved Larry from the moment I saw him, but it wasn't an easy decision. This was only three weeks after I walked out on my first husband."

"So what happened?" Andrea asked.

"Everyone was telling me I was being stupid, that I should think about what I was doing." She paused again. "That I was rushing into it, that it would never last."

She paused again to get her breath. Looking directly at Andrea, she added.

"But sometimes, life is about taking risks. If you plan your life, you can only live in the future, not the present."

Sally turned to look directly at Andrea.

"And I remembered the words of that old lady, so Larry and I got married soon after."

"That was fifty-six years ago, and not for one single day, have I ever regretted that decision."

She paused again and took a deep breath.

"So when I saw you sitting on the same bench as I did, I knew I had to come over. To see if I could help you and repay the kindness that old lady had shown me and the wise words she had spoken."

She hesitated momentarily. "I do have to go now as Larry will be wondering where I am, but it would be nice to see you again. I live at number 24, just over there," she said, pointing towards the street.

Sally slowly got to her feet.

"I would like that," Andrea replied. "Very much."

Sally took a few steps, turned around, and smiled once again. A smile that seemed to indicate that everything would be all right.

***

She watched Sally walk away, slowly moving each stick in turn until she disappeared from sight.

Sitting for a long time, Andrea watched people go in all directions. Some just ambled along enjoying the evening, some hurrying with a look of determination on their faces. She couldn't help feeling they all seemed content with their lives.

She felt empty and lost in a city of over eight million people. She had wasted years of her life with Jim.

If only she could be like Sally.

Chapter 9

Rob

Monday 14th September

He slipped out of bed quietly, anxious not to disturb Claudia. Although her breathing sounded heavy, she wakened easily.

He felt a knot in his stomach whenever he thought about his birthday party. So much for sharing a quiet evening with Claudia. He also had to share it with Jeff. But now, his thoughts focused on the photograph.

Sitting at the kitchen table, he took another sip of coffee, his eyes fixed on the photograph. The photograph his mum kept hidden for over half a century. He had so many questions. Why hide it? Was she ashamed of it? If so, why did she ask about it? Did it remind her of a bad time? Maybe she just wanted to be reminded of when she was young. Maybe it reminded her of his dad.

He was just about to pour himself some more coffee when, to his surprise, he could hear Claudia coming down the stairs. His body reacted with an involuntary intake of breath, feeling the tension in his stomach. The last time she had drunk too much, she had stayed in bed most of the morning.

Opening the kitchen door, she headed directly towards the coffee pot, avoiding any eye contact. Walking slowly, she looked pale with dark circles under her eyes.

"I'll get coffee for you," he said.

"No," she replied, her voice raspy. "I'll get it myself."

Holding her coffee, she walked tentatively over to the opposite end of the table and sat down, keeping her gaze on her coffee mug.

"Are you okay?" he asked.

"I really don't want to debate this now," she said. "But you embarrassed me last night. And then you just fucked off with the feeble excuse you had to take your mum home."

"I know. I'm sorry," he said. "I really am."

She took a sip of her coffee, keeping it in her mouth, her cheeks expanding before she swallowed it.

"You know we can't go on like this," she said, still avoiding any eye contact. "It feels like I'm living with a stranger at the moment. And I won't go on like that."

She was just about to say something else when she noticed the photograph on the table.

"And what's that? What have you been looking at now?" she asked accusingly.

He pushed it over to her.

"Who is… oh wow… is that your Mum?"

"Yes, in New York, when they lived there," he replied. "She's been asking for a while if I'd found a photograph, but I didn't know what she was talking about."

"She looks so... beautiful, despite the orange fading. Imagine what it looked like when it was first printed."

"She looks happy?" he asked.

"Yes."

"I was going to see if I could get hold of the negatives and get it reprinted."

"What?" she replied. "After fifty years?"

"I thought it was worth a try."

"It's up to you," she said dismissively. "But I think you're wasting your time."

They both sipped their coffee in silence.

"Anyway," she said, pausing momentarily. "I'm not sure how to say this, but I've been thinking about this the last couple of days." She paused again.

Her tone was making him anxious.

"It's now been a full year since you lost your dad, and I know it was a massive shock." She hesitated as if trying to find the right words to say.

He sensed there was a but coming.

"But, whenever I try to talk to you, it seems like you're on a different planet. I don't recognise you anymore." She hesitated momentarily. "I know I haven't always been patient, but I've done my best to help you through this but…"

Here we go, another but.

"We can't go on like this," she added.

"Have you finished?" he asked

"Yes," she replied tersely.

He had been staring at her while she was talking but now shifted his gaze downwards to his coffee cup.

"It's all about you," he replied quietly. "As usual," he added.

"No, it's actually all been about you," she shouted. "How much you've suffered, your terrible loss… oh..."

He stared at Claudia in disbelief.

"Rob, I'm sorry," she said softly. "I shouldn't have said that. I didn't mean it."

He sensed she was about to speak, but he put his hand up a second time.

"It's my turn," he said, his voice low and controlled.

"You've no idea… none…"

She was about to reply, but he put his hand up quickly to stop her.

"My dad is dead." He paused, desperately trying to keep his emotions in check. "He was killed by your friend's sister. She thinks it was just an unfortunate accident. It wasn't." He paused momentarily. "She conveniently forgets it was her sister who killed my dad," he paused again. "Because she was driving carelessly. And yet, you still invite her into our home."

"But it wasn't Maggie who was prosecuted," she protested. "It was her sister. Anyway, it wasn't proven his heart failure two days later had anything to do with the crash. As a lawyer, you know that already."

"There you go again, defending your friend and her sister," he replied angrily. "Why do you feel the need to defend your boss' wife and her sister?"

"It's been a year, damn it," she responded sharply.

"Huh?" he said, interrupting her. "Are you going to say that it's time I moved on?"

"Well, yes," she said, stuttering.

"Not once have you asked me recently how I actually feel?" he replied. "You couldn't be more insensitive if you tried."

He watched her get up slowly, glaring at him.

"If you think that," she shrieked. "Then go find somebody else who can be more sensitive to your needs."

She kicked the chair back and went to storm out of the kitchen.

"Wait, let's talk?" he asked.

She spun round to face him.

"No," she replied abruptly. "I'm going back to bed, then I'll get a shower," she said, trying to keep herself under control. "After that, I'll be in the study, but I want to be left alone."

As he listened, he felt the guilt tightening his stomach, almost making him nauseous. He had tried to make things better with Claudia but instead, he had made it even worse.

"Okay," he said as she slammed the door behind her.

He could hear her moving around upstairs, and despite everything, he loved her. But he knew that saying it was not going to be enough. Somehow, he needed to demonstrate it.

Picking up the photograph, he studied it closely. A thought suddenly came to him. If his mum had gone to have her photo taken, then surely his dad would have gone with her. If so, there could be a photograph of both of them.

He had a growing conviction that uncovering what seemed to be a mystery about the photograph would help him deal with losing his dad. But more than that, it could also save his marriage. Apart from anything else, he had nothing to lose.

He picked up the phone and called his senior partner at the office.

Chapter 10

Claudia

Monday 14th September

The spare bedroom overlooked the back garden with the large magnolia tree directly in front of the window. Sitting at her desk, it was a sight that both delighted and inspired her. Well, usually, it did.

Looking down at the blank screen on her laptop, she felt despondent. Desperate to block out the problems with Rob, she needed a distraction.

For the past hour or so, she had typed words but then deleted them. However hard she tried, the right words would not come. Jeff had told her he needed her article by the end of the day. That was now looking unlikely.

Although she had been distracted dealing with Rob, she had started to feel the passion that had once consumed her had started to wane. She had started to feel the pressure of the deadlines, which, in turn, made it harder for her to write anything.

Despite her throbbing head and feeling a little nauseous, she had to get the article written. Leaning back in her chair, she turned her gaze outside, taking in the magnificent magnolia tree with its knobbly seedpods which next Spring would reveal a beauty that would dominate the garden.

She glimpsed blue patches of the sky, now starting to appear between the clouds, promising a reappearance of the early morning sun.

Her student days came into her mind when her idea of excitement was spending an evening, sometimes all night, writing. Closing her eyes, she could see herself sitting at a small desk in the corner of her room, the words flowing out of her. Again, she could feel the immense satisfaction of writing the last word of any submission.

Opening her eyes, quite inexplicably, she felt a surge of internal energy, her mind focusing on new possibilities, refusing to be constrained neither by the past nor the present.

She felt invigorated.

At least for now, the burdens of the past few days no longer dominated her. Replaced instead by a new hunger, an enthusiasm that had too often evaded her recently.

Her fingers moved to the keyboard, moving across the keys, words flowing freely. As the phrases, sentences, and paragraphs revealed themselves on the screen, her mind and thoughts were stimulated even more.

For three hours, she worked, stopping only to get coffee. Otherwise, she blocked out everything else. She heard the phone ring, but that was not her task today.

Finally, she fell back in her chair, exhausted but exhilarated.

She felt satisfied that the article was finished, and she was ready to hit send.

But before that, a short message to Jeff.

Sorry for the long delay, but here it is.

My best and my last work.

Speak to you soon.

Claudia

Gazing at the words she typed, she knew this was the right step.

All she had to do now was to tell Rob.

***

Rob

"Okay, that's great, thanks," he said as he put the phone down.

This will prove to her that I am really doing something to move on.

Hearing Claudia come down the stairs, he needed to see her. He had some good news.

"Are you in the study?" she called.

"Yes," he replied.

She opened the door. "I have something to tell you," she said excitedly.

"Well, I have—"

"I've just resigned from the magazine," she blurted out, interrupting him.

"Oh."

"I've just emailed Jeff to tell him."

"Oh."

"Is that all you have to say, oh?" Showing her annoyance at his lack of support.

It wasn't that he wasn't supportive, just stunned at the news.

"So what are you going to do instead?" he asked curiously.

"Write a book."

She paused, waiting for a response, but he had nothing to say.

"You know that already. I've mentioned it before."

"Okay, that's great, if that's what you want," he replied, trying to recall any earlier discussion.

"Oh, my god," she said, exasperated. "Don't be too pleased for me, then."

"I am," he replied, but clearly with insufficient enthusiasm for her.

She seemed to forget she showed zero interest in his picture mystery. Her tone turned accusatory when she didn't get the response she wanted.

"Anyway, why are you not at the office?"

"That's what I wanted to tell you. I've taken the week off. I'm owed a week."

"Oh," she replied.

"You were right. I do need to deal with my father's death. I can't explain it, but finding that photo reveals a part of their lives I really didn't know about before."

"Sorry, I'm confused," she replied sarcastically, her hands on her hips "How is finding a single photograph going to reveal anything about their lives back then?"

He just stared at her, wondering why she was being so dismissive.

"Because there must be more than one photograph. And if anyone's got them, it will be the photographer."

"So you find several photos instead of one. So what? They are all going to be similar."

"Well, yes," he replied, knowing she had a point. "But if I get the negatives, I can get it reprinted for Mum to look at. It may help her memory."

"I'm not sure about any of this," she said. "Anyway, it does sound a bit pointless."

"And," he added, ignoring her barb. "He may even remember

mum and dad."

"Get a grip," Claudia said sharply. "This all happened over fifty years ago. Even if he or she is alive, how on earth are they going to remember taking pictures that long ago?"

Aware that she was glaring at him, he looked down at the photo laying on his desk in front of him.

"I think it's worth a try," he replied quietly, still avoiding eye contact "I need to do this." he added.

She looked at him, shaking her head.

"I've already made several calls to New York trying to get their contact details, but no luck. I was just going round in circles, but it was suggested that it may be more productive if I went over there instead." He hesitated. "I've booked a flight leaving at four today."

"Have you lost the plot?" she asked, staring at him with her mouth half open.

"It's important," he replied softly. "I need to know about that picture. It's pointless asking Mum. I… just need to know."

"Do what you want. You will anyway," she sneered. "I've already said that you'll be wasting your time, but clearly, you don't want to accept that. This is just you running away from everything."

He stepped towards her.

"Maybe a break will be good for both of us?" he suggested.

But she did not answer and turned to leave the room.

"I'll take you to the airport," she said flatly as she walked away.

***

Back in her study, the phone started to ring.

"Claudia?"

Recognising the voice, she answered, "Hi Jeff, how are you?"

"What on earth do you mean, your best and last work? You can't just quit like that. You just can't," he said, clearly agitated. "You're a terrific writer. Just because you have been a bit slow in getting a few articles to me, that doesn't mean you have to stop altogether. Why don't you—"

"Jeff, will you stop for a minute, so I can say something?" she asked, trying to keep her voice calm. "There is something I want to do, and I can't combine this with the magazine."

"But—" Jeff started.

"And before you try," she said, again interrupting him. "You will absolutely not change my mind, so can we now drop the subject… please?"

"Okay," Jeff replied. "But what is it that you need to do that is so important?"

"I have always wanted to write—it all goes back to my uni days. If I don't do it now, I never will."

"Listen, can I pop round to see you?" he suggested.

"Why? There's nothing to discuss."

"Oh, come on, we've worked together for nearly seven years. We can't just finish this in just one phone call. Or I can take you out to dinner?"

"Listen, I'm exhausted, so why don't you and Maggie come round this evening, and I will make something simple if that's okay with you?" She continued. "Rob is off to New York this evening, so I probably can do with the company, anyway."

"Fine with me," Jeff replied. "Would seven be okay?"

"Sure, but remember, I'm not going to change my mind."

"I know, I know," he replied genially.

Slumping back into the chair, she promised herself she would not give in to him.

***

Walking into the kitchen, Rob said, "I'm ready."

"Okay, let's go," she replied. "I'll drive."

They barely spoke as they headed for the airport, even though the silence made the journey uncomfortable. With the airport coming into view, Claudia cleared her throat.

"You know, sometimes I don't feel I really know you anymore and… I'm sad about that."

Rob had his head down. "I'm sorry. I know I keep saying that, but I'm not sure what else to say."

"I know," she said, adding, "I know you're struggling, but don't forget I am as well."

"I know," he replied.

"And please don't forget about next Saturday," she said.

"What?" he replied, looking directly at her.

Her eyes were on the road ahead, but she could feel his eyes on her.

"Nicky."

"Oh yes," he replied dismissively. "The wedding."

"Yes, and I've already told you the theme is dance, as she's a professional dancer." She paused. "And you agreed to take some lessons."

"Okay, okay," he said impatiently. "I'm just surprised you have to remind me now about this bloody wedding."

"I'm just saying."

"Yeah, and I'm saying I'll try to be back."

Claudia stopped the car right outside the main entrance to the departures hall.

He leant over and kissed her on the cheek. She flicked a smile but stayed silent.

After retrieving his bags from the boot, he headed for the main doors.

She watched him briefly, waiting for him to turn around to wave as he always did. She felt she was losing him, that he might never come back. Feeling tears welling up, she put the car into gear and sped away.

***

Rob turned around to wave to her, just in time to see the car disappear. They had always exchanged that final wave whenever he went away.

Turning back to head to the departure gates, he could only feel a horrible emptiness inside.

Chapter 11

Andrea

Monday 14th September

Exhausted after a long restless night, she was relieved to see the clock reach 6 A.M.

Pushing the tangled blankets aside required effort, but she willed her feet to reach the floor. It felt strange Jim not even being in the apartment. Sometimes, if they argued, he would sleep in the other bedroom, but not this time.

Needing coffee, she shuffled around the bed, but her reflection in the mirror made her stop. Seeing her disheveled appearance made her feel worse.

"What's wrong with me?" speaking to her reflection. "Why can't I be content with what I've got?"

Sitting at the kitchen counter, a steaming mug of coffee clasped protectively in her hands, she kept replaying the argument in her mind. But it was the conversation with Sally where she felt a resonance with what she had told her.

"Maybe it's time to go home," she said, talking to the empty room.

Despite her fatigue, she had to go to work, almost welcoming the distraction it would offer. Heading down into the subway, with the unmistakable smell of pastries and coffee, and a blur of people running in all directions, she started to pick up the energy of the city.

The train could be heard in the distance, and with a gust of wind, it arrived at the platform. After three loud beeps, the doors opened. Seeing a carriage with fewer people, she entered it. Seconds later, the train was on the move.

Twenty minutes later, she readily embraced the cool air greeting her as the office building doors moved aside for her. Then, needing water, she headed to the staff room.

Standing, filling her cup, she hears Babs chatting in the corridor. The last person Andrea wanted to see, particularly today. As section supervisor, she had a reputation for being rude. If you were on her media team, you were fine. Anyone else, she tended to ignore.

"Hi, Andrea. Thanks for showing up," she said sarcastically.

"But I'm not late," Andrea responded softly.

"You're paid to work at your desk, which started five minutes ago, not to get water," Babs replied dismissively as she walked away.

"Just ignore her."

Andrea spun around to see Julia was walking towards her.

"You know she's a bully," Julia said. "At least she's not our supervisor."

"Thanks. She's always been off with me, probably because I'm just a temp."

"I guess so. Anyway, you look awful," Julia said, wiping up a spillage by the coffee machine.

"Gee, thanks. To be honest, I feel awful."

"Don't tell me… Jim?"

"We've had a bad argument, and he walked out and hasn't returned. He went to a friend's and told me I needed to move out." Andrea replied, trying not to be emotional.

Putting her arm around her, Julia said, "Oh honey, I'm sorry. I'm sure he doesn't mean it. It will work out if you want it to work out," Julia said sympathetically then picking up her coffee, Julia turned to leave. "Let me know how it goes, okay?"

"Thanks."

The morning dragged by. Working through lunch, Andrea kept her mind occupied, but she kept drifting back to the argument, wondering if Jim had gone back to the apartment. Would he say he didn't mean it? The more she thought about it, the more she convinced herself he would come back, and they could sort it out.

Midway through the afternoon, Babs rushed into the office.

"Sorry, I was rather brusque with you this morning. It's so crazily busy," she said, sounding more abrupt than apologetic. "Anyway, would you like a trip to the airport?"

"Um… when?"

"Now. Someone else was going, but they've gone home ill, typical. It's a simple job. All you have to do is to meet the client off the flight, the 4 P.M. from London. Give him this folder. He has a connecting flight to Charlotte and needs to have this with him. Now, you need to keep this with you all the time. It's an original script for a news documentary. You lose this, and you lose your job. Got it?" Turning to leave. "Did you get that?" Babs asked.

"Yes," Andrea replied, bewildered as she hadn't agreed to go, let alone potentially lose her job.

"Then go. Oh, I'm happy if you want to get the cab to take you straight home after. It's probably not worth you coming back to the office. But don't forget to keep the receipts," she said as she walked away.

Andrea sighed deeply. This was the very last thing she wanted to do.

Standing outside on the sidewalk's edge, her eyes were focused on the traffic racing down the street, searching for a vacant cab. She was relieved when one pulled up alongside her. Yanking the door shut, she settled onto the torn, spongy seat and caught the lingering odour of curry.

She looked around the cab.

Typical. I had to flag down and get the dirtiest and smelliest cab in the city.

Arriving at the airport, Andrea checked the arrivals board. The British Airways flight from London had already landed, but the passengers had not come through. Seeing the arrivals area, she headed over, dodging people all rushing in different directions. Breathing a sigh of relief, she took up a position, with her sign giving the name of her legal firm.

"Excuse me," someone asked. "Have the passengers from London come through yet?" Before Andrea could reply. "I'm waiting for my son," she said, smiling.

Feeling the lady was a little overcome with the busyness of the airport, she said, "I don't think so. I'm waiting for someone as well. Why don't you wait next to me?"

"Oh, thank you, my dear."

The doors to the baggage area swung open, and another swarm of passengers came towards them. Some were only focused on locating the exits, others looked lost and confused, and others were scanning the boards being held aloft by drivers.

As they passed her, she scanned their faces closely, but none looked in her direction for more than a glance. By now, the old lady had gone, happily reunited with her son.

Apart from his name, all she knew was that he was over six foot tall, in his early fifties, with dark hair. Then the doors opened again, and several people came through. She watched one man who she was convinced was the client. He was tall, with dark hair, about the right age, wearing dark jeans and a white shirt.

Looking lost, she watched him closely and headed in her direction. "Excuse me," she asked. "Are you Mr Marshall?"

The man looked confused. "Sorry, no," he answered politely. "But can you tell me where I can get a cab?"

"Oh, sorry," she replied, feeling embarrassed. "You can get a cab through those doors."

She watched him as he headed towards the exit door, still fascinated with his wonderful English accent.

"Hello, I'm John Marshall." The low, confident voice said suggesting he was well-educated.

Andrea quickly swung back around.

Standing directly in front of her. "I think you have something for me?" He asked, smiling broadly.

"Um... yes... sorry." Pausing briefly. "I didn't see you there."

"No, I didn't think you did. I just guessed it was you. There are not too many people holding a thick folder."

"Here you go," she replied, feeling a little flustered.

"Thank you so much for meeting me. I really appreciate it."

Still smiling, he headed off towards the departure area. Feeling annoyed with herself for not noticing the client sooner, she walked over to the line of yellow cabs.

She looked around briefly, but the Englishman was gone.

Jumping in the first one, she was pleased it bore no resemblance to the earlier cab. It was delightfully clean with the smell of new leather. Shouting out her address, she settled into her seat. As the cab approached the mid-town tunnel, the splendid view of Manhattan revealed itself, but she was now lost in her thoughts.

Would they be able to sort their relationship out? She did love him despite his outbursts. Did he really mean it when he said it was over? He'd said that before but then later said he was sorry.

"Here you go, Miss."

Andrea was so lost in her thoughts she hadn't noticed the cab had stopped right outside her apartment. If she did move back home, she would miss the apartment. She loved the large airy rooms of the red brick building. Opening her apartment door, she breathed a sigh of relief. She was just about to pour herself a glass of water from the cooler when her phone rang.

"Hi, Mum," she said, pressing the speaker button.

"What… I'm not your mum," Julia said, laughing.

"Oh god, sorry, my mum normally phones me on a Monday evening, so I just assumed it was her."

"Quite funny," Julia replied. "Anyway, just wanted to check you were okay?"

"I'm okay. I'm just back from the airport."

"Yes, I heard," she replied, laughing.

"He's not here, but he normally has basketball on Mondays, so he could be back later."

"So, what are you up to?"

"Well, don't laugh, but I did book a course of dance lessons. Someone in the office was talking about it a few weeks ago. I'm not sure if I really fancy it now."

"Don't be silly. You really should go," Julia replied.

"Maybe, but I'll see you tomorrow, and thanks for the call."

The line went dead.

Realising she needed to take back some control, she decided to go.

Chapter 12

Rob

Monday 14th September

It had taken a little over eight hours, and now, for the first time in his life, he was in New York. He was following in the footsteps of his mum and dad, who had made the same journey over half a century earlier.

Despite warnings of lengthy queues at US immigration, he had collected his bag, and within twenty minutes, he was in the arrivals area.

People were rushing in different directions, chatting in languages he had never heard before. Habitually, he scanned briefly the faces of those waiting for arriving passengers with the unrealistic expectation of seeing a face he recognised.

Apart from a girl who seemed to be watching him rather suspiciously, there were none. She even approached him, thinking he was someone else. But at least she knew where he could get a cab.

Pushing through the crowd, he headed off to get a cab, then noticed the huge taxi sign over the top of the main exit doors.

Emerging outside, the warm, humid air was thick with a raft of different smells. With the line of waiting cabs extending as far as he could see, Rob pulled out a piece of paper with the address of the photography shop. As he did so, a cab pulled up alongside him. Greeted only with a nod, the driver waited in silence, strumming his fingers on the steering wheel.

Settling into his seat, he handed over the piece of paper.

"Vacation or business?"

"Um… a bit of both, I guess," Rob replied.

"So you looking to stay here?" Holding up the paper.

"No, why."

"Well, the area's a bit run down, and there's certainly no swanky hotels."

"No, just checking something out before I get to the hotel," he replied, preferring not to get into any discussion. Before he could fasten his seat belt, the cab pulled away at speed.

But the question about being on vacation troubled him. And he knew why.

Perhaps Claudia could have come with me. But she didn't, as I never asked her.

As they sped down Midtown Expressway, he gazed out the window at the ever-changing scenery. Up ahead, the skyline of Manhattan came into view. He had seen so many pictures of Manhattan, but seeing it right in front of him for the first time, took his breath away.

"Mum and Dad have seen this," he said under his breath.

"What's that?" The cab driver asked.

"My parents lived in New York before I was born. This is my first visit… and what a great view."

"Well, enjoy, as it will disappear in a minute. We're heading down the Midtown tunnel."

As the skyline of the city slowly disappeared from view, he pulled out, for the umpteenth time, the photograph he had in his pocket. This was why he was here, he reminded himself, smiling at the image of his mum.

Emerging from the Midtown tunnel, the noise of the city filled his head, the sound of car horns every few seconds, people shouting at each other, the pure randomness of the place. From the big, swanky skyscrapers to the shops and other buildings that seemed to have been standing since the beginning of the century, none seemed out of place. He could feel the energy of the city even from the back of the cab.

As they got closer, he could feel his anxiety grow.

What if Claudia was right? What if this is all a complete waste of time?

Rushing along 34th Street, bouncing over the uneven road surfaces, the smell of freshly cooked food from the pavement food carts seeped into the cab. Opening the window, the aroma got stronger, but the ever-present stench of exhaust fumes pumped out by the endless flow of cabs was never far away.

In awe, he gazed up at the famous Empire State building standing proudly above 34th Street, dwarfing the surrounding buildings, the pavement crowded with people seemingly all in a rush.

"Just a few more blocks."

A few minutes later, the cab slowed and then stopped.

"Sorry, Buddy, but the street's shut off. I can't go any further. You'll have to walk."

Darkness was coming sooner than he expected. He briefly considered returning in the morning, but he was close now, too close.

"Which way?" he asked

"Go to the end of this block. Take a left. That's the street you want."

Grabbing his bag, he handed some dollar bills to the driver.

"Good luck," the driver said.

Within seconds the cab had disappeared.

The driver was right. The area had clearly seen better days. Most of the buildings seemed residential, although hardly any seemed occupied. Several youths rode up and down the street on skateboards, played basketball, or drank. Feeling rather over-dressed, he felt a little anxious, telling himself this wouldn't take long.

With the humidity still high and already feeling hot, he felt his shirt had now become permanently attached to his skin.

Turning left at the end of the street, he was dismayed when he saw it was little more than an alley. Each side was lined with what looked like shop units, many of which were boarded up, all daubed in graffiti.

Walking slowly down the alley, he studied each frontage carefully, trying to find number 102. He could find numbers below twenty, but that was it. In despair, he threw his bag onto the ground and slumped down on the steps leading up to one of the boarded buildings. He had flown 3,500 miles for nothing. Claudia was right, and Mary was right. It had been a stupid idea.

But for now, he just wanted to get to his hotel and get showered. He needed to think this through.

Wiping the sweat from his head and neck, he picked up his bag and headed back to where the cab had dropped him. He was just a few yards away when he heard a shout.

"Hey, flash guy, what you doing round here?"

Rob swung around to see three youths walking towards him, probably in their late teens. One of them swinging a baseball bat.

"Just getting a cab," he responded, continuing to walk away.

"Stop there," one of them shouted.

He kept walking, but then he heard one of them running after him. Thinking he had no choice, he stopped and turned to face them.

The leader, who was about the same height as Rob, stood directly in front of him. Rob could feel his heart pounding.

"Give us your cash, or my buddy here will smash your knees."

Before he could respond, a voice boomed out from somewhere behind them.

"Get away from him, or there'll be trouble… got it?"

As soon as the youths recognised who had shouted at them, they immediately turned and ran back down the street, disappearing around the corner. Rob felt he was about to have a heart attack, with his heart pounding away in his chest and his hands and arms trembling.

"It's okay, buddy," the gruff voice behind him said. He turned around. "They wouldn't have hurt you… well, I don't think so," he said, smiling.

Rob looked at him sceptically.

"Are you okay?" he asked

"Just shaken up a bit," Rob replied, his voice wavering.

"Oh, sorry, I should have introduced myself. I'm Manny. My place backs onto this street," he explained, pointing to a nearby building.

With his gruff New York accent, he looked to be in his fifties. Slim and only around five feet six, his deep voice didn't seem to match his body.

"I'm Rob."

"This area is being redeveloped. In the meantime, the thugs have moved in, shame, really."

"I thought I was in trouble," Rob interjected.

"We're used to it. They know my brother's a cop. Anyway, what you doing round here? You a Brit?"

"It's a bit of a long story, really."

"Why am I not surprised? Listen, you look a wreck. I own that dance school, well, it was my mum's. I run it now, come inside and have a seat. I think you need it."

"I can just get a cab," Rob replied.

"No, I wouldn't hear of it, come in and get a drink, at least."

Rob reluctantly agreed and followed Manny towards the back door of the dance studio.

"Here for a vacation?" Manny asked as they walked together.

"Well, sort of."

"Interesting response." Manny replied, looking at Rob curious-ly.

"Welcome to Sylvie's Dance Studio," he said, smiling as they walked in the door. Pointing in different directions, Manny said, "This is the main studio. That way are two small studios, and over there are the changing rooms and a kitchen. Grab a seat, and I'll get some iced water for you."

Dropping his bag on the floor, Rob collapsed in the nearest seat, breathing a sigh of relief.

Spread around the room's perimeter were a wide variety of chairs, from old bar stools to small sofas. Floor-to-ceiling mir-rors covered the whole of one side of the room, and a set of parallel bars was against the far end of the room. The opposite side of the mirrored wall was covered in rows of photographs along with shelves holding medals and silver trophies.

So this is what a dance school looks like?

Rob smiled to himself.

If Claudia could see me now.

"Here you go." Handing Rob a glass. "I have a class in 45 minutes."

Rob could hear footsteps coming up the stairs.

"In here," Manny shouted.

A man with a shaved head, probably in his late forties, burst into the room. Wearing a black tee shirt and jeans, he seemed to have the same demeanour as Manny.

"This is Rob. I rescued him from those kids. You need to go and have another chat with them before they actually hurt someone," Manny said to the man.

Then looking back at Rob, he said, "My brother, Charlie."

"Our Mum taught us both to dance. We didn't really have much of a choice, did we?" he said, looking at Charlie. "But we lost her three years ago, and I took it over."

"I'm probably the only cop in the whole of Manhattan that can dance," Charlie responded in a low, gravelly voice. "I still get teased, but actually, it doesn't bother me."

"So Charlie helps me out when I'm short of male partners," Manny added.

"I was always keen to learn as I always wanted to be an actor," Charlie said, smiling. "Not sure how I ended up being a cop instead."

"You told me earlier you had a long story to explain why you were loitering in our neighbourhood," Manny said. "So what's your story, or are you really up to no good?" he continued, teasing him.

"It's not really that interesting, really. I don't want to bore you," Rob replied.

"You won't. Go ahead."

Rob mentioned the photo, that his parents had lived in New York but that his dad had died and his mum had dementia. And finally, his reasons for wanting to track down the photographer.

Manny and Charlie listened intently. When Rob had finished, they stared at him in disbelief.

"But that's over fifty years ago. Not exactly an easy task," Charlie said.

"All I can say. You Brits don't really like to do things the easy way, do you?" Manny said.

"I guess not."

"We can certainly ask around for you," Charlie said. "But we can't promise anything, but if, and it's a big if, this photographer is still around, I'm pretty sure we can find him for you."

"Charlie's right," Manny agreed. "We'll do our best to help, but you need to help me out first."

Charlie and Manny exchanged glances.

"Oh," Charlie said, grinning.

Starting to feel worried, Rob wondered if he should just leave.

"It's not bad," Manny said, laughing.

Pointing to Rob's case, he asked. "Do you have a change of clothes in there?"

"Yes," he said, suspecting something.

"Can you dance?"

"Definitely not."

Charlie had his mouth covered, trying to control his laughter.

"I have never danced in my life. Although I was supposed to go to a dance class with my wife this week, I've come here instead."

"Interesting," Manny said.

"Before we do anything else, can I suggest you go and get a shower?"

"What? Now?" Rob queried.

"Trust me," Manny said. "You definitely need a shower."

Chapter 13

Rob

Monday 13th September

After the traumas of the afternoon, Rob yearned to get to his hotel, if only to get something to eat. But Manny had offered to help find Grossman, so it was worth the wait.

As he packed away his dirty clothes, he noticed his wallet had fallen open, and a smiling Claudia was looking up at him. Picking up the wallet, he wondered what she would think if she could see him now.

He would phone her later and tell her about everything that had happened, although she probably wouldn't believe him. He could hardly believe it himself.

"Well, you almost look human now," Manny said, standing in the doorway.

"Thanks," Rob replied. "But do I really need to do this?"

Manny smiled. "It's dead simple. Just listen to everything I say, Charlie will be next to you, and he's a pretty decent dancer for a cop, so just watch him."

He followed Manny into the main studio, where the students had already started to gather. With every step, Rob felt increasingly nervous.

"Grab a seat. It won't be long," Manny said. "And stop worrying."

Taking a seat, he just wished the whole evening was over.

***

Andrea

Andrea saw the sign for Manny's as she walked up the street. Even by New York standards, it was an old shabby-looking building, and it occurred to her that it may be better just to go home. But to what?

"No, let's do this," she said to herself.

As she opened the door, three other aspiring dancers followed her up the stairs towards the dance studio.

"This place is a dump," a voice behind her muttered quietly.

"Shush," another voice replied. "It's not a dump, it's one of the oldest dance schools in Manhattan, and some famous dancers came here."

"Well, I'm guessing they're all dead now."

"Quit moaning. We're here now. Anyway, you're the one who wanted to try something new."

Andrea listened to this exchange and couldn't help smiling to herself.

As they all reached the top of the stairs, Manny, smiling broadly, emerged from the studio to greet them.

"Welcome, ladies. Please go straight through," he announced in his booming voice.

The atmosphere in the room seemed a little tense, with inconsequential polite conversation trying to disguise everyone's nerves. Feeling self-conscious, Andrea hesitated before walking into the room. Seeing spare chairs at the far end of the room, she walked quickly towards them.

Although the cool air was a welcome relief from the humidity outside, she was convinced she could detect a faint smell of sweat.

Now seated, she looked across the room, noticing two older men sitting by themselves.

This is going to be awful. Simply awful.

Andrea switched her attention to the three aspiring dancers who had settled themselves in the corner of the room, piling up their jackets and bags on one of the chairs. The group comprised a guy in his thirties, with long dark hair and an equally dark beard, a blonde girl with dimples who was possibly his partner, and an older woman with similar features to the younger girl. Andrea made up her mind she was the girl's mum.

The blonde girl couldn't be more excited and was clearly taking this all very seriously.

"What are you doing?" the guy asked, watching her get other shoes out of the bag.

"I'm putting my dance shoes on."

"Oh," he replied in surprise. "I didn't realise you had any."

"I bought them yesterday," she responded in a tone suggesting that it was in no way premature to buy dance shoes even before she learnt to dance.

The guy sighed. It was clear he really didn't want to be there.

"Look," the blonde girl announced, pointing to some photos on the wall. "I told you some famous dancers have been here."

"I don't recognise any of them," the young guy replied dismissively, barely glancing at them.

Glaring at him, she said, "Will you please give this a chance?"

Her patience starting to wane. As she was speaking, Manny walked into the studio.

"Okay, welcome. My name's Manny."

As soon as he started to speak, everyone turned to face him.

"This is the first of three classes over the next three evenings. Tonight, we're going to learn the waltz. We're going to start with some very basic steps so you get used to moving your body in a different way."

"Any questions?" he asked, making the question sound rhetorical.

Manny scanned the room.

"Okay, can you all stand in one line facing me, don't worry if you don't have a partner. We have two spares."

"There you go, they've got a man for you, Mum, the blonde girl announced.

Mum was not overly impressed.

Charlie was now walking towards them.

"Hi, this is my Mum," she announced to Charlie. "She needs a partner. Mum, come over here."

Andrea had assumed there was no need for partners. She noticed the taller one hadn't moved, he seemed okay, but she was now giving serious thought to leaving herself.

But it was too late. He was now walking towards her, looking nervous. Admittedly, he didn't look as creepy as the other dance partner, but she felt uncomfortable.

The other one probably had sweaty hands and bad breath. Yuk.

She just wanted the evening to be over.

***

Rob

"The girl at the end, the pretty one with the dark hair," Manny said. "She seems a bit shy, so be nice."

Rob hesitated.

"Go then, dance time. What are you waiting for?"

Feeling anxious, he walked reluctantly towards the pretty girl with dark hair. This was going to be a disaster. Perhaps he wouldn't tell Claudia about this bit.

"Hi, I'm Rob," he said, trying to sound confident. "I'm your dance partner, not that I have ever danced before."

The young woman stared at him, her mouth partly open.

"I'm sure Manny could find somebody else to be your partner if you prefer," he said, sensing her reluctance.

"No, sorry, it's just you look sort of familiar. Have we met?"

"I very much doubt it."

"Were you…?" she wondered if she had seen him at the airport, but he would be at a hotel, certainly not here.

"No, forget that… anyway, I'm Andrea," she said.

Before he could respond, Manny's voice boomed out.

"Okay, everyone," Manny said. "Can you all stand side by side, facing me, but make sure you have enough room to turn without bumping into those next to you. Some warm-up steps to start with. Feet together and concentrate on moving together. Take one step to the left and then bring your right foot to touch your left. Take another step left and bring your right foot together. And now back again, starting with your right foot."

Determined to get the steps right, Rob became fixated on his feet.

"Keep going," Manny instructed. "Well done, well done."

Looking at Manny's face, he wasn't convinced he actually meant it, even though they had gone through the sequence several times.

"Okay, time now to try some very basic waltz steps. Guys, you first, watch me."

"Good luck," Andrea said.

"Thanks, I'll need it," Rob responded tentatively. "I'm Rob, by the way."

"Step forward with your left foot," Manny instructed. "Then step to the right with your right foot,"

"Now close your feet by bringing your left foot next to your right. Now step back with your right foot. Step left with your left foot. Lastly, close your feet by bringing your right foot next to your left."

Rob sighed audibly, not realising he had been holding his breath.

So far, so good.

"A couple more times and then… ladies… it will be your turn."

It was all going well until the final run-through. Instead of moving his left foot, he moved his right and stumbled.

Feeling embarrassed, Rob kept his head down, hoping no one noticed.

***

Andrea

"Now, ladies, your turn, but the steps are slightly different."

She had been watching Rob closely. He seemed to be trying really hard and felt she needed to do the same. Okay, he made a mistake at the end, but actually, he was quite good. She was still plagued by the thought that he was the guy at the airport. He certainly looked the same.

"Good luck," Rob said.

"Thanks. I'll do my best not to trip up," she said, smiling.

Manny's voice boomed out again.

"Okay, ladies. Let's go."

"Step back with your right foot. Then step to the left with your left foot. Now close your feet by bringing your right foot next to your left. Now step forward with your left foot. Next, step right with your right foot. Lastly, close your feet by bringing your left foot to your right. Excellent," he called out.

"A couple more times, and then you will try this with your partner. Okay, stand facing your partner."

Feeling apprehensive, Andrea looked across at an even more worried Rob.

"I'll try not to step on your toes," Rob said.

"Likewise," Andrea replied with a grin. Hesitating slightly, she added. "By the way, if you can't dance, why are you acting as a dance partner?"

"It's a long story, a very long story."

"Okay, everyone, listen up," Manny shouted, interrupting their brief discussion.

"We're not going to use the proper hold tonight. I just want you to stand facing your partner and place your hands on their shoulders."

They moved closer to each other and took up their position.

"I hope I haven't got bad breath," Rob ventured

"Oh, did you have curry earlier?" She asked.

"Oh no. Why?" he responded, thinking he had bad breath.

"Just kidding," she replied, giggling.

"I may have to stand on your toes for that," he replied, smiling broadly

Manny walked close to them. "You need to get a little closer to each other. You will find it easier."

Andrea took a small tentative step towards him. Now only a few inches away, she could feel the warmth of his body even before she touched him. As he placed his hands on her shoulders, she felt her skin tingle as if a feather had touched her. Raising her arms, she laid her hands on his shoulders, immediately feeling the dampness of his skin through his shirt.

A short time ago, they had never met, but now, she felt there was perhaps a bit of connection between them but at the same time, she sensed Rob felt a little uncomfortable.

"Okay, now to the music."

The voice of Elvis Presley singing *Are You Lonesome Tonight* started to resound around the room.

"Okay, get ready."

Despite her earlier reservations, she was now feeling a little more comfortable. She didn't know this guy, but she felt strangely safe. Even with Jim, she had never really felt like this.

Charlie leant over to Rob. "Watch me." He nodded in response.

Manny's voice boomed again throughout the room.

"Feel the rhythm 1-2-3, 2-2-3, 3-2-3… okay after three, 1,2,3..."

After each step, she felt more confident. Their feet moved side by side, toe to toe, in not quite perfect unison.

"Guys, don't look down at your feet. Look up," Manny shouted.

"Look lovingly into your partner's eyes."

Seeing Rob whip his head back up, Andrea giggled.

Unintentionally pulling her closer to him, his eyes held hers for a beat too long. It felt suddenly very intimate. In that second, she saw kindness in his face but also a trace of sadness.

Throwing her head back a little, she laughed, breaking the awkward eye contact.

He chuckled along with her, causing his concentration to be lost. Taking a wrong step, he stood on the toes of her right foot.

"Ouch," she yelped, suddenly breaking away from him.

"Sorry," he blundered, feeling the room grow hotter. "Are you all right?"

Bending down to feel her toes. "I think they're broken," she said, wearing a serious expression.

"Oh my god, I'm…."

"I'm kidding," she said, smiling.

It took him a second to take it in. "Oh, very funny," he said, now grinning.

"Good one," Charlie remarked, who had been watching them.

"Let's try again," she suggested.

Rob nodded. Taking up their positions, she again felt his hands back on her shoulders. This time, a little more firmly. Picking up the steps again, they both quickly fell back into the rhythm of the music.

"You're pretty good," she whispered. For a second, their eyes met again. In that moment, she wanted to tell him how wonderful he made her feel, how the past few days had been awful, and he had given her fresh hope. But before the words could be formed, Manny spoke, and the moment passed. Not that she would have said them, anyway.

"Well done, everyone," Manny shouted, turning the music off. "That step is called the box step. Just remember all other steps in the waltz are based on that movement. It's always at the count of three. That's it for tonight. Same time tomorrow evening."

"Thank you, I hope I wasn't too rubbish for you," Andrea said.

"Not at all, and sorry for standing on your toes," he replied. "Will you excuse me? I need to speak to Manny."

"No worries," Andrea responded, watching him walk over to where Manny was standing.

In the meantime, the three aspiring dancers had packed up their bags and were heading towards the stairs. The blonde girl was buzzing with excitement. The other two just seemed glad to be leaving.

***

Rob

"Well done, everyone," Manny shouted.

Breathing a sigh of relief, Rob headed to the door. The girl, Andrea, was nice, but she seemed to like eye contact, which made him feel a little uneasy.

"Hey, buddy." Manny's voice boomed as Rob approached him. "Thank you," he started. "You did a great job. I know we sort of forced you, but hopefully, you enjoyed it. You seemed to," he said smirking.

"Sorry, why the smirk on your face?"

"Come on, that girl was flirting with you. Gazing into your eyes, and you gazing back."

"I was not gazing back," Rob retorted.

"Okay, if you say so, anyway, I've got some good news about your photographer."

"Seriously?"

"Yep, I made a few calls before class and happened to strike lucky. A mate of mine used to own a diner a couple of blocks away. He knew Grossman quite well. Apparently, he went in there every day. Back then, this was a real nice area. Anyway, Grossman lived above the photography studio, but when he retired, he moved to another apartment. I've put the address on here," Manny said, handing him a card.

"My mate thinks he moved out of New York a couple of years ago but doesn't know where. He suggested you go to his old apartment as the tenant may know where he went. But go round in daylight. Some people don't like answering their doors at night."

"This is great. Thanks, Manny."

"Actually, I did find it before class," Manny admitted. "But I thought if I gave it to you, then you would disappear," he said, smiling.

"Probably," Rob replied with a nod.

"Good luck. If you fancy another dance lesson, come along tomorrow night," he said.

"I'll see how I get on," Rob replied. "And thanks again for all your help."

Picking his bag up, he headed off down the stairs, feeling relieved to be finally on the way out of the place.

"Hey, dance partner." Surprised to hear her voice, Rob swung round.

As they reached the bottom of the stairs, she asked. "So, did you enjoy it?"

"Yes, sure. How about you?" he asked.

"Actually, it wasn't as bad as I thought it would be. I really didn't know what to expect. Listen, I just wanted to say sorry for being so miserable earlier. It's just that I am struggling with something at the moment and, to be honest, I nearly didn't come but... I'm glad I did.

"Oh, don't worry about it," Rob replied. "I didn't actually plan to attend the dance class. I was, sort of, persuaded to participate."

"Really?" she said with surprise. "Why were you persuaded?"

"It's a long boring story. It's just that I am looking for someone."

"Really?" she replied excitedly.

He noticed her staring at his bag and couldn't help wondering why.

"Well," she said. "If you need help to track anyone down, just let me know. I'm an amateur sleuth."

"Really?" he replied quite intrigued.

"No, not really, but I think I would be good at it."

"Oh, I see. I'll bear you in mind, I think," he replied, smiling. "But I do need to go. After a flight from London and an unexpected dance class, I'm looking forward to getting to my hotel."

"Oh," she almost screamed. "It was you at the airport."

Rob stared at her, and then he remembered.

"Of course... I asked you where I could get a cab," he replied incredulously. "That's a heck of a coincidence."

"It sure is," she responded.

She seemed desperate to ask more questions, but it didn't spill them.

"Maybe see you at the next class?" she asked.

"Maybe," he responded. "Maybe."

***

Andrea

She watched Rob hail a cab and slump into the back seat. After the profoundness of meeting the old lady on the bench, meeting The same guy from the airport at the dance class shook her. She'd never felt so optimistic that the universe was trying to tell her something. Andrea had no clue what that might be, but she hoped she would see him again.

Chapter 14

Rob

Monday 14th September

Settled in the back of the cab, he felt a palpable sense of relief, but the image of the youths threatening him with a baseball bat still haunted him. He kept reminding himself that nothing actually happened, but the anxiety persisted.

Manny's comment about the girl with dark hair was ridiculous. Yes, she did seem to want some eye contact, but that wasn't flirting. It was just about trying to be on the same wavelength for the dance steps. She was clearly nervous, as he was, so it helped.

The dance lesson certainly wasn't as bad as he thought it would be. In fact, he quite enjoyed dancing or at least trying to dance. Perhaps, if he had another lesson, he would be able to at least dance a few steps with Claudia at the wedding. He wanted to do that for her, although he wasn't sure if he wanted to return to Manny's.

Looking at the card in his hand, he smiled to himself. At last, he had a starting point for his search.

As he looked out the window, the city seemed to change every few minutes as the cab raced through different areas of Manhattan, bouncing violently as it went. Stopping at some traffic lights, he noticed a woman who must have been in her seventies, with dirty, tangled hair and a torn plain dress, shaking a tin can. Within a couple of minutes, the cab had moved on, passing some upmarket stores. He felt it strange how two opposite ends of society seemed to merge so effortlessly together yet were a million miles apart.

He just stared as the cab slowed and stopped outside his hotel.

Now he realised why the rate was so reasonable. Being New York fashion week, most hotels were fully booked. Eventually, he managed to find one, and now he knew why. No one else wanted it! Maybe the room itself will be okay, but he doubted it.

The lobby was sparsely furnished, with several wicker chairs scattered randomly opposite the reception area. The receptionist, a small, lean guy, wore a crumpled white shirt under a navy jacket that appeared to be at least two sizes too large for him.

Looking no more than fifteen, he greeted Rob in a voice that could only be described as strangled.

"Hello, can I help you?" he asked.

"You have a room for me. My name's Watson," Rob ventured.

"Oh yes, it's all ready for you. We didn't think you were coming. But delighted you have made it."

Handing Rob the key, he added. "And it's one of our top rooms."

Following his directions, he headed to his room, encouraged by being allocated one of the best ones.

Perhaps this will not be so bad after all.

Opening the door to his superior room, he said out loud, "Oh no."

It was dark and dingy even with the lights on. There were two single beds that had been pushed together, covered with a dark burgundy cover with a circular design. There was a well-worn dark brown striped carpet and brown floral curtains. It was a depressing sight.

He dropped his bag on the floor and slumped on the bed, exhausted.

With the room door firmly locked, he actually felt safe for the first time since arriving in the city. Too tired to empty his bag, he just removed his clothes and slipped into bed.

The day's events spun around in his head for a while, but he pushed them away until exhaustion took over. He desperately wanted to speak to Claudia, but it was too late. He would call her in the morning, but he wouldn't tell her about the dance lesson, not just yet. He wanted to surprise her at the wedding if he could. With Claudia in his thoughts, he closed his eyes and fell asleep.

Chapter 15

Andrea

Monday 14th September

Andrea watched the cab travel up the street until it disappeared around the corner.

She loved walking down 6th Avenue towards her apartment. But tonight, she was oblivious to the city. Despite herself, she had enjoyed the dance class, and for the first time since Jim left, the aching hollowness just didn't seem as bad. With each step, her mind became clearer and more resolute than ever before to move on. Sally was right. She had to follow her heart, Jim wasn't coming back, but more importantly, Andrea knew she had to move on. She needed to focus on her future. But she needed something else, to make changes and time to work out what to do. In the meantime, the dance classes were fun, and she decided she would return for the next lesson.

But she couldn't get her mystery man out of her head. He wore a ring indicating he was married, but why was he by himself. Maybe he was not who he seemed to be, maybe she needed to avoid him, his behaviour was a little odd, and she was convinced it had something to do with his bag. But despite, or perhaps because of, her misgivings, her curiosity became more intense. She seemed to recollect one of her crime stories which depicted a villain carrying a hold-all around with stolen cash and a gun that had been used in a murder.

Maybe he was one of those eccentric English guys, but then again, he didn't seem to be eccentric. The mystery continued to deepen. She needed to know, but it was too late. She had missed her opportunity to find out more.

And now, she would probably never know.

Although it was getting late, the humidity still lingered. As Andrea walked, she could feel the dampness seep through her white blouse, making it cling to her back.

Standing outside her apartment, she held her breath, not knowing whether she wanted Jim to be there or not. Opening the door, she felt a sense of relief when she saw the room was in darkness. Putting the lights on, she closed the door and double-bolted it. She kept reminding herself that she needed to put Jim in the past, but it was hard. She still felt that dark emptiness within.

Sitting at the kitchen counter with a glass of cold water in her hands, she stared at the clock. Seconds ticked deafeningly by. Had Jim known when they got the clock? Had he known when they brought it home, struggling to lift it up the stairs, and hung it over the exposed brick fireplace?

Her stomach ached at the thought. Drawing her knees up, she closed her eyes, trying not to hear the clock or the silence cut through.

But she hated the silence. Perhaps it was growing up in the city. The silence was unnatural in the city. It felt like something particularly bad was about to happen.

A loud screeching sent her jumping off of her stool. Water splashed over her legs as the phone on the counter trilled again.

"Hello?" Andrea said nervously.

"I'm sorry," Jim said softly. "I really am."

Hearing his voice made her gasp.

"It's not your fault. It's mine," he continued. "I didn't mean to say those things."

"Jim...."

"Andrea, let me talk. I need to tell you something," he paused, and she heard him take a sharp intake of breath. "I just can't tell you this face to face."

Andrea could hear Jim breathing rapidly as if he had been running.

"I've not been honest with you. I've not been honest with myself." His voice trailed off.

She felt her body stiffen.

"Honest about what?" she replied, growing anxious. "Just tell me, what's wrong? I don't understand."

"I've met someone," he replied flatly.

Andrea felt like she'd been punched in the stomach. She tried to speak, but no words would come.

"Andrea?"

Although she could feel tears welling up, her hurt started to translate into anger.

"You mean you have been seeing her behind my back? Have you... have you?" Andrea retorted, her voice rising. She felt she was about to explode. "Who is she? Do I know her?" She was screaming down the phone at him.

Jim remained silent.

"Jim, tell me, I need to know, damn it," she insisted.

There was a pause.

"I'm gay." His words seemed to hang in the air.

"What?" Her first inclination was to laugh.

They had been together for some time. How on earth could he be gay? That was impossible.

"What did you say?" Thinking she had misheard him.

"I've been denying it to myself for a long time, but I can't anymore," he said.

But his voice seemed to lack any sign of regret, which irritated her.

She was still shaking with anger.

"So you've just been using me all this time."

"It wasn't like that. I love you," he replied softly. "That's why I kept deferring the question of getting married. I think I always knew this day would come… and it has. I am so sorry. I have been trying to tell you, but it never felt like it was the right time. I guess there would never be a right time. I do love you, but if I stayed, I know I would be unhappy and possibly end up resenting you. I am so sorry. Hopefully, one day, you will understand."

Andrea listened intently, but to her, it was just words.

"All I know is that if you really cared for me, you would've been honest. But you just lied," she said, trying hard to keep her voice steady.

"I'm so sorry," he said. "I really am."

"So… um… what happens now?" she asked, feeling confused. "We've been together for nearly two years, and now you decide you never wanted me in the first place."

"It's not like that," he responded.

"So, after all this time, you are kicking me out?" she asked angrily. "Just like that."

"Of course not. I'll stay with my friend for the time being, so you don't need to see me."

"Oh," she replied. "It's like that, is it?"

"It's not like anything. I thought it would be easier for you."

"You mean easier for you. Don't worry, I'll get out of your way so you can live your new life… without me."

"Thank you," he replied.

"So what's your friend's name then?" she asked sarcastically. "No, don't answer that." She sighed. "I don't want to know, and one last thing, I never want to see you again. Ever."

Andrea slammed the phone down.

Her life had been shattered, and as much as she tried to hold it in, the pain came out of her in a heart-wrenching wail. She picked up the phone and threw it across the room, tearing it out of its socket.

Sitting at the kitchen counter, she was angry, but the rejection hurt her most. She felt used, empty, and numb. She had wasted two years of her life with him. Then, she crumbled as reality hit her. As much as she tried to hold it in, the grief came out of her in a heart-wrenching wail. Struggling to hold back the tears, they came anyway, flowing steadily and silently down her face. A lone tear traced down her cheek and then another until they streamed from her already puffy eyes, dripping like rain on the kitchen counter. Her desolate sobbing punched through her as if she was being hit in the stomach. She hung her head down until it rested on the kitchen counter, and there she stayed until her crying eventually subsided.

Chapter 16

Andrea

Tuesday 14th September

With the arrival of the morning, she found her bed to be cold and lonely without him.

Slowly and reluctantly, she removed the bed covers from her face but closed her eyes again. Memories of pleasant dreams were fading away fast, being replaced by harsh reality, and with its arrival, the return of a familiar ache within her.

Jim had been pretending all along. "Why didn't I see this coming?" she said out loud. "Why didn't I challenge him about our relationship? Why all this pretence?"

She had laid on her bed for what seemed to be hours, longing for sleep to consume her. Exhausted and emotionally drained, she had eventually fallen asleep.

She tried to lie still a while longer, but her body was forcing her to move. Begrudgingly, she got up and went into the kitchen. Her mouth was dry, and she yearned for coffee.

She had promised to meet Julia for lunch, but as she was not going to work today, she needed to phone her.

"It's me," she said when Julia answered. "I'm not in the office today, but can we meet for lunch? Usual place and time?"

"Um, sure. Are you…?"

"Not now. I'll tell you about it when we meet." She said, interrupting Julia.

"Oh, okay," Julia replied, seemingly surprised by Andrea's unusual curtness.

Without saying anything more, she hung up.

Since Sunday, she wondered where she had gone wrong. Andrea blamed herself for Jim walking out on her, but that all changed when Jim came out last night. She had known her relationship with Jim had never been perfect, but she always thought it was her fault. He never liked her spending time reading her crime books and was only able to read them when he was out. She hated him for stringing her along yet at the same time, but she now realised this would have been hard for him. She didn't know if she hated him or felt sorry for him. Either way, her life was a mess, and she needed to resolve it. Feeling sorry for herself was not going to help.

They met outside the Plaza Hotel and headed towards the park. Crossing the sidewalk into the park was like going into another world. One minute, surrounded by skyscrapers and then replaced by large trees, some of which were there years before the larger skyscrapers.

On the way, they hardly spoke, almost an unsaid silence. Julia would normally be doing all the chatter, but sensing Andrea's hurt, she kept quiet. After picking up some lunch, they walked to the Mall, a walkway lined with trees on both sides, reminiscent of some of the parks in England, recalling some pictures she had seen.

They found an empty bench just under some trees, glad to be out of the glare of the sun. No sooner had they sat down, the questions came as Andrea had expected.

"So honey, what's this all about?" Julia asked softly. "Tell me what's going on?"

Andrea had her head down with her eyes fixed on a small flower that had forced its way up between some stones. It was alone and vulnerable to be trampled on by walkers, yet it had survived so far. Andrea felt like that flower, alone and vulnerable with an uncertain future.

Struggling to find the right words, Andrea hesitated, took a deep breath, and let it all out.

Julia sat open-mouthed and listened. As she spoke, tears flowed, and the pain and frustration raged within, but she carried on. She needed to talk.

And then she fell silent.

"Honey, I am so, so sorry," Julia said, holding her close.

"Did you not have any idea?"

"No, he acted strange at times, but I never questioned him. I assumed it was me." Pausing for a moment. "The thing is, I've wasted two years of my life, and he never ever wanted me."

"So what are you going to do?" Julia asked gently.

"I've decided I am not going to let him win," she replied as she wiped her eyes.

Julia looked at her curiously, wondering what she was about to say.

"I know I have to get past this. I know this sounds odd, but I met an old lady a couple of days ago, just after the argument with Jim, who told me to follow my heart. I've been wondering ever since how that applies to me." She hesitated slightly. "I've decided to go back home, to San Francisco. I only stayed here this long as Jim said he wouldn't ever leave the city."

"I thought you liked New York?" Julia asked.

"I do," Andrea retorted. "But I need a fresh start. To be honest, my parents were never really happy that I was with Jim. They met him a couple of times, but I could tell they never really liked him."

"But what are you going to do for a job?"

"No idea. I haven't got that far yet. I'm staying with my parents to start with, but I do want to get my own place, so I need to get a job. Maybe with one of the local newspapers. I've always wanted to do it, but I don't know, I sort of got distracted."

"By Jim," Julia retorted

"Maybe."

"So, a new you. I think that's amazing."

"No," Andrea hesitated momentarily as she thought about it.

"The me, I should always have been."

A natural silence fell between them.

"When do you go?"

"This weekend."

"What?" Julia responded, clearly shocked. "You do move fast."

"I phoned the Personnel Manager before I came to meet you. I explained everything, and she agreed I could leave immediately, although I need to go in tomorrow to hand over any files I've been working on."

"Well, I have to say I'm impressed."

"Not sure I will get everything packed up in time. Do you think I'm doing the right thing?"

"Well, only you will know that," Julia replied.

"Julia," she uttered nervously.

"That sounds ominous," she replied.

"I need to do one last thing. I need to close a door before I can move on."

Julia looked at her curiously.

"Will you come with me?"

"I guess so," she said, glancing at her watch. "To be honest, I've overrun lunch already, so what the heck," she responded. "What do I need to do?"

"This is very likely to be the last time I will be here, in Central Park, I mean. Maybe I'll visit in the future, but there are two places I would like to see again now, but I don't, or rather can't, do it by myself."

"What are we waiting for?" Julia said with a trace of a smile.

"I'll explain on the way. Ever since I moved to New York, Central Park has always been my favourite place to go. It felt like being in the country without leaving the city. And because it's so vast, it's quite easy to find solitude." She paused momentarily. "But this is also where I met Jim."

"Here." Pointing towards the Wollman Rink just ahead of them. "I was at the ice rink with a girlfriend from the apartment next door, I was so clumsy, I kept falling over."

Andrea paused, reliving the moment in her head. "Jim was working in the skate school, I took a tumble, and he helped me up. For the next half hour, he taught me how to skate properly. He was lovely and kind."

Again, she paused.

"As I was leaving, he came over and asked if he could call me to go out together. Without thinking, I said yes. The following morning, he called, and we met that evening."

In silence, they kept walking for a couple of minutes. Andrea noticed that Julia wasn't her usually chatty self and she was grateful.

"He brought me here, to this Carousel. I had passed it before when I was in the park but didn't take much notice. We had an incredible time." Her voice cracked.

Taking a deep breath, she continued.

"It was the largest merry-go-round I had ever seen. And Jim knew all about it. How many horses there were, I think it was over fifty, and they were all hand carved."

The Carousel had been closed temporarily for maintenance, but the horses were still visible. Julia stayed motionless while Andrea walked by herself towards the Carousel. Reaching forward, she touched one of the horses, then immediately turned around and returned to where Julia was standing. Julia looked at her, registering the tears were flowing gently down her cheeks. As Andrea came close, Julia put out her arms and hugged her.

"Have you reached that point yet?" Julia asked.

"What do you mean?"

"When you will start to follow your dreams."

"Yes, that's why I had to do this today. I had to close this chapter in my life. To say goodbye to it. So thanks for being here."

"I'm guessing I won't see you again before you go."

"Probably not."

"I'll miss you," Julia said.

"And I'll miss you," Andrea replied, wiping her tears away.

Chapter 17

Rob

Tuesday 14th September

Despite being the worst hotel bedroom he had ever been in, he had slept soundly. Opening his eyes, it occurred to him the room actually looked better at night. Checking his watch, he picked up the phone. After several rings, she answered.

"Hello," Claudia answered apathetically.

"Hi, it's me," he replied. "Sorry I couldn't call last night. It was late before I got to the hotel."

"I see," she said curtly.

"Listen, I know you're annoyed with me but let's not be distant with each other."

"Well, you're the one that left to trip off to the other side of the Atlantic."

"I know." He acknowledged. "But I'm making some progress."

Claudia stayed silent.

"And it's positive."

Still no response.

"You still there?" Rob asked.

"Of course I am, I'm not exactly over the moon with what you're doing, but I guess I just need to accept it. You say positive. Does this mean you are feeling more positive?"

Taken by surprise by the question, he hesitated, knowing he needed to reassure her.

"Um, yes," he replied. "I know you thought this trip was insane. Yesterday, I would have agreed with you. But I'm finding out more about Mum and Dad's life over here. I've no idea why it helps, but it does."

"So what happened yesterday?"

Rob told her about the experience of seeing New York for the first time, about not finding the photographic studio, and that he had an address for the photographer. He decided not to mention the mugging or the dance lessons.

Claudia did not comment.

"I'll call you tomorrow," Rob ventured. Hesitating momentarily, he added, "I love you."

But it was too late. She had already hung up.

***

After grabbing some breakfast at the diner next door, he headed for the address Manny gave him. Despite his initial excitement about finding the photographer, an underlying anxiety remained. If he was going to have any chance of saving his marriage, he needed to show his trip to New York had been worth it.

Getting closer to his destination, there were parts of New York where he felt it was like being in the middle of a film set, particularly when they passed the brownstone buildings that had been standing for decades and were symbolic of the city. If he ever lived in New York, he thought it would be there, not that a move to New York would ever be likely.

"This is it," the cab driver announced.

In many ways, it was just an ordinary building, but it had a certain style that made it look impressive. It was a five-storey building with tall, narrow black-framed windows. Against the front of the building was the familiar cast iron fire escape that cascaded down the brick and stone façade in perfect Zs. The front entrance was up eleven wide, lightly coloured stone steps with black painted handrails on both sides that flowed towards an impressive wide black front door.

With a degree of apprehension, he walked slowly up the steps. There were four rows of buzzers, and he pressed 'Apartment 4a'. There was no response. After waiting a few seconds, he pressed again but still no response.

Perhaps they were out. Perhaps they've gone to work.

He tried again. Still no response. Feeling disappointed, he turned to go back down the steps. He would try again later.

At the same time, a woman in her early sixties, wearing a red and white checked dress that could be seen from the other end of the street, was walking up.

"Excuse me, I wondered if you could help, I'm trying to contact the occupiers of apartment 4a."

"Why?" she replied curtly, looking at him suspiciously.

"I'm trying to locate the photographer that used to live here a number of years ago."

"Really? And why would you be looking for him?" she replied brusquely.

Rob hesitated briefly. "He took a picture of my mother, and I would like to get the negatives so I can get it reprinted for her," he answered, wondering why she was asking.

"He retired years ago, so you're wasting your time," she replied impatiently, walking past him.

"But did he live here? His name was Mr Grossman," Rob pressed.

"You are persistent, aren't you?" she replied. "Yes, he did used to live here, but they moved out of the city about four years ago, so you're wasting your time."

Her voice getting louder.

Rob kept pressing, realising this was his only opportunity to find out more. The stakes were too high to walk away now.

"I'm really sorry, but this is really important to me. My mum has dementia. My parents both lived in the city a long time ago. I got this address from the guy that runs a diner near Sylvie's Dance Studio."

"Well, I can't say I ever heard of Sylvie's Dance Studio," she retorted. "I assume you're British?"

Rob pulled out his passport and showed it to her, hoping it would persuade her to help.

"Okay, you win, but I'm not sure I can help too much."

"Do you know where he moved to?" Rob asked hopefully.

"Gee, you don't give up, do you?"

"As I say, it's important."

"Yea, yea," she replied. "I get it."

She thought for a moment.

"Okay, wait here. I'll see if I can find it. Not sure I still have it. Anything to get rid of you," she replied with a sly grin.

"Actually, why don't you come up? My husband will be back soon, anyway."

The apartment was on the second floor overlooking the street. Although the entrance hall was quite dimly lit, the apartment was bright and airy.

"Okay, wait here, pointing to a chair by the window. I will need to see if I can find it."

It wasn't a large apartment, but it was well-furnished. The lounge had two big tall windows covered with white lace curtains. Just off the lounge, Rob could see a kitchen and then another couple of doors leading to, he assumed, a bedroom and a bathroom.

He couldn't help feeling anxious. If she didn't have a forwarding address, what was he going to do?

"Okay, I found the file, so that's a start," she said as she walked back into the room. Her voice was more friendly.

She placed it on the table next to him and slowly flicked through the various pages.

"Can I ask your name?" she asked as she studied the various papers.

"Rob… Rob Watson."

"I'm Brenda," she replied, still looking at the papers.

"Ah, I have found a number. Not sure if it still works, but let's try it."

Picking up the phone, she dialled the number. Rob could barely contain himself.

But then she put the phone down.

"Well, the number still seems to work, but there's no answer."

"But this is it," she said, handing the piece of paper to him.

Rob held it as if it was worth a fortune.

"Thanks for trying."

"Oh wait," Brenda said, still looking back at the file. "I have a mail forwarding address, but it's a mailbox, so it may not be too much help."

"That's terrific, thank you," Rob said excitedly.

"All I can say," she added. "Is that it must be a very special photograph."

Hesitating slightly, Rob replied. "It is… it's very special."

Walking away from the apartment, he felt a sense of excitement. He now had a phone number and a mailbox address. He felt he was getting closer. Deciding to walk some part of the way back to the hotel, he headed towards the end of the street, arriving at 10th Avenue. Approaching the corner of 10th Avenue, he felt he was being hit with a wall of noise. Heavy trucks rumbled up and down. Cab drivers impatiently hit their car horns. Behind him, groups of people chatted and laughed.

Full of noise and full of energy. He did feel positive, even invigorated but wished Claudia was with him. They could have enjoyed this experience together. But perhaps she wouldn't have wanted to come.

On the corner stood the Empire Diner. Although he had never been there, it looked familiar. In need of coffee, he headed inside. In front of him, his eyes focused on the vast menu on the wall, then down to the food counter, storing most of the menu items in three rows of polished metal-covered containers, illuminated under bright heat lamps. He was unaware of how hungry he was until now.

He ordered eggs and toast.

"Over easy or sunny side up?" the server asked.

"Um, sorry?"

The server chuckled.

"Do you want the egg flipped over in the pan?"

"Oh, yes, please."

Now I know what over easy means, Rob thought as he headed to an empty table by the window.

Gazing out at the busyness of the street, he wondered if his mum had walked this street whilst his dad was at work. Perhaps they had both been in this diner. Perhaps his mum did like New York. He was really looking forward to seeing her again when he got back, hopefully with some other photos.

After eating his over-easy eggs, he noticed a payphone in the corner of the diner. He dialled the number but again, no reply. With a growing sense of frustration, he decided to head back to the hotel.

As the day was cooler with far lower humidity, he started to walk up 10th Avenue, embracing the vibrancy and buzz of the city. The people walking past him fascinated him, so many faces, so many nationalities, all seemingly in a rush to be somewhere, but all belonging to this amazing city. He wondered if his mum and dad felt they belonged here.

Chapter 18

Rob

Tuesday 14th September

He had spent most of the afternoon redialing the number. After each unanswered phone call, his frustration grew. Having been in his dreary hotel room for most of the day, he was now desperate to get outside.

Perhaps Manny might be able to help? Or even the girl from the dance school, unable to recollect her name.

Checking the time, he realised he would need to leave within the next five minutes to get to Manny's dance class on time. Closing the door behind him, he was just about to rush off down the corridor when he heard his room phone ring. Quickly retrieving his key, he rushed back into the room, but it stopped before he could answer it.

If it's important, they'll leave a message.

Relieved to be outside, he felt invigorated by the cool evening air. A cab was coming down the street, and seconds later, he was seated in the back, headed for Manny's. The cab took no more than ten minutes, but the journey was awful. Not only did it smell of stale food, but the seats were also torn, and the floor was full of old food containers and other disgusting items, which he chose to ignore.

"Well, look who's here, guys? It's our British friend, the one who likes baseball," Manny announced, laughing at his own joke.

"So you here for the dancing?" Charlie asked.

"Or the girl with the dark hair?" Manny said teasingly.

"Very funny," Rob replied. "I figured I might have another lesson, but I was also after some advice."

He told them he had a mailing address as well as a phone number. He had tried the number most of the day but with no success.

"That's frustrating," Manny said. "Maybe they're away?"

Manny turned to Charlie. "Can you find out the residential address from somewhere?"

"Not possible, I'm afraid. Mailing box addresses are convenient, but individuals can keep their real addresses private. Sorry Buddy."

"Oh,"Rob replied, trying to shake off the feeling of disappointment. But he had come this far and wasn't about to give up yet.

***

Claudia

After taking a sip of wine, she dialled the hotel number Rob had given her. She regretted how she had spoken to him earlier and needed to apologise. Despite everything, she really missed him.

Waiting to be connected by the hotel operator, she felt apprehensive about how he would be with her.

"Sorry, Ma'am, the line's engaged, any message?"

"No. Thank you," Claudia replied.

Well, at least he's in his hotel room.

Suddenly, the front doorbell rang, making her jump. Feeling guilty, she went to open the door, but she already knew who would be there.

"Oh god, I'm so sorry, Jeff. I meant to phone you to postpone."

"Oh, no problem," he replied. "Is everything okay?"

"Where's Maggie?" she asked.

"At home, she's fine," he replied. "It's just her bloody back again. She just needs to rest it. I tried to phone and left some messages, but I guess you didn't pick them up."

"No, sorry, I've been out all afternoon," she replied, still feeling guilty. "As you're here, why don't you come in?"

"No, it's no problem. I'll go, but we do need to chat at some point."

"I know," she paused. "But we might as well do it now."

Claudia led the way into the kitchen.

"Have you eaten?" she asked. "Although I can only really offer you a sandwich."

"Sounds good," he replied.

"To be honest, I've had a bit of a lazy day and couldn't be bothered cooking, so I bought these prepacked sandwiches. Hope they'll be okay."

"Sounds perfect to me," Jeff replied. "How's Rob?"

Hearing Rob's name made her hesitate. "To be honest, it's all been a bit strained since Saturday. And now he's gone off on a mission to find a photographer in New York."

Clearly puzzled, Jeff asked, "What photographer?"

"Sometimes, I think he's losing the plot," she replied. "But I'm worried about him." She added. "Actually, do you mind if I try to phone him? The line was busy earlier, but he should be in his hotel room."

"Of course."

She went into the hall, picked up the phone, and hit redial. Waiting again for the hotel operator, she had a feeling he wouldn't be there.

"Sorry, ma'am, there's no answer. I've tried a couple of times. Any message?"

"No thanks," Claudia replied anxiously.

"It's odd." Speaking to Jeff as she walked back into the room. "There's no reply now, and it's getting late. I can't think where he will be."

***

Andrea

She poured some iced water into her glass and took a sip. Sitting down at the kitchen counter, she subconsciously started strumming her fingers. She allowed herself a rueful smile as Jim always got annoyed whenever she did that.

Although still unsure about attending the dance class, she knew she needed to get out. And her calendar wasn't exactly full, and she couldn't help wondering if Jim would show up.

She happened to look at the clock, suddenly realising she only had twenty minutes to get there.

"Come on, move, let's do it," she said out loud to herself. Ten minutes later, she was in a cab and after another ten minutes, walking up the stairs to the dance studio.

Approaching the door to the main studio, she looked around. Everyone seemed to be there. More in hope than expectation, she looked around for her mystery man. When she didn't see him, she felt a pang of disappointment, which surprised her.

"Hello." Hearing a familiar British accent, she swung round. He seemed different. Wearing a light blue shirt with chinos, he looked far more relaxed than the previous evening.

"I didn't know if you were coming tonight," he said.

"To be honest, I wasn't sure myself until half an hour ago."

"Okay, everyone, take up your positions exactly like last night," Manny shouted as he turned on the music, interrupting their conversation.

"Oh no," Andrea said. "Elvis Presley again."

"Clearly, Manny's favourite," he replied.

The one-hour lesson seemed to pass quickly. They rehearsed the Waltz steps over and over again with Elvis all the way.

"I'm exhausted," Rob announced at the end.

"Likewise, but I thought we would learn some other dances," Andrea whispered.

"To be honest, it suits me," he replied. "I'm supposed to be dancing with my wife at a wedding next weekend."

Andrea swallowed hard. That was the first time he had mentioned his wife. She told herself she was being stupid. She already knew he was married.

"Are they friends of yours getting married?" she asked.

"Oh no, Claudia's, she's my wife," he replied.

Again, his response shook her.

He had just used his wife's name. Well, of course, he used her name. That's her name, so why wouldn't he use it?

She started to question why she was even talking to this guy or arguing with herself. Just say goodnight.

As they were walking down the stairs, he turned towards her.

"Can I ask you something?"

"Of course," she replied, a little nervously.

"When I told you last night I was looking for someone, you said you could help?"

"I did, didn't I?" she replied hesitantly.

"To be honest, that's why I came tonight. I hoped you would be here."

"So it wasn't my wonderful dancing then?" she said, teasing him.

"Oh well," he replied. "That goes without saying."

"Good response, so how can I help?"

"As I mentioned, I'm trying to find someone, but all I have is a mailbox address and a phone number. I've been phoning the number all day, but there's no reply. Just wondered if you had any ideas on how to find out the residential address."

The fact that he had not given her any reasons for wanting to find this person intrigued her.

Why was he keeping this secret?

With a sense of hopeful anticipation. "I'll try to help, but why do you need to find this person, if you don't mind me asking?"

"It's a long story," he replied.

She felt he was still trying to deflect her.

"Maybe, but I would still like to know."

"Of course," he replied.

"Okay, how do you feel about going to get a coffee and you can tell me your long story?" she said with a trace of sarcasm.

He seemed surprised by her suggestion, and she wondered if she was being too presumptuous.

"That's fine if you've got the time," he replied.

"Oh yes," she replied. "I've got plenty of time."

She immediately regretted making that comment, but he didn't seem to notice.

"There's a diner over there," she said, leading the way enthusiastically.

Julia will never believe any of this.

***

Claudia

"Maybe he's gone out to get something to eat," Jeff proffered.

"Maybe..." Claudia replied but was not convinced.

She went on to tell him about the photograph and why he had gone to New York.

"And he just wanted to go by himself," she added. "Can you believe that?"

"I'm so sorry," he replied. "This must be really hard on you."

Reaching for the wine, she topped up both their glasses.

"So what's this all about giving up your column?" Jeff asked, changing the subject. "I thought you enjoyed it?"

"I did, I do, but I have always wanted to write a book, something permanent."

"But you have said this—"

"Yes," she said, interrupting him. "I have said this before, but twelve months ago, you know what happened. It put everything on hold. Quite frankly, Rob is not interested in anything I want to do." She stopped abruptly. "Sorry, I shouldn't have said that. But unless I do this now, I probably never will."

"I can understand that," he replied. "The idea of writing a book is certainly fascinating. What's the story?"

"Women's human rights. I'm not sure yet how I will approach it but most likely, I will try to include it as a novel's storyline. Hopefully, it will then have a wider appeal."

Jeff was listening intently.

"You know, so many people talk of writing a book," Jeff said. "But only a small percentage actually do it," he said, looking directly at her. "I would say you are in that small percentage."

Pausing momentarily, he added. "I believe in you. I always have. That's why I will miss you from the magazine."

"Thanks for saying that," she replied. "I just wish Rob felt the same."

Staring at her glass, she asked, "Can I tell you something?"

"Of course," Jeff replied. "I'm your friend now, not your boss."

"I keep thinking I should leave Rob." Her voice cracked.

"But why?" Jeff asked, shocked by what she had said.

"Because he's not the man I married. Sometimes he seems like a stranger to me. It's been a year, a whole year, Jeff."

He stayed silent.

"He's not asked one question about the book," she continued, her voice reflecting her hurt. "He's totally disinterested and doesn't care. When I dropped him off at the airport, he just walked off and didn't even bother to wave goodbye. If it wasn't for Amy, I probably wouldn't be here now."

"Oh, I'm so sorry, Claudia," Jeff said. "I didn't realise it was that bad."

"And I feel so guilty for even thinking like this," she added.

Jeff moved closer, putting his arm around her to comfort her.

"I'm sorry, Jeff. I shouldn't be telling you all this rubbish."

"You're a friend. You can tell me anything," he replied. "You are one amazing lovely person."

"At least someone appreciates me," she said.

Claudia felt Jeff move closer to her, placing his hand on hers, which she found strangely comforting.

"I'll always appreciate you," Jeff replied.

As he spoke, he leant into her and brought his lips to hers, kissing them lightly. Feeling the stubble of his beard on her face increased her desperate need for affection. A warmth consumed her as she leaned into the kiss, Jeff's lips firm against her own.

She put her arm around his shoulders, pushing her body even closer. Jeff kept gently kissing her.

"Shall we… ?" he whispered against her mouth.

Hearing the question and knowing what he meant, immediately caused her to hesitate.

"Oh no," she yelped as she jumped up and backed away from him. "This should not be happening. Oh god, this is so embarrassing. What a mess."

"It's okay," he replied. "I'm a devastatingly handsome young athletic, bronzed guy, so I understand," he said, trying to lighten the mood.

"It's not a joke," she said sharply. "Please go, please?"

Picking up his jacket, he walked out of the room. Hearing the front door close, she breathed a sigh of relief.

Why did she do that? And why did he take advantage of her? He said he was a friend. Friends don't do that.

"What have I done?" she said out loud.

As she spoke, Rob came into her mind.

I wonder what he's doing now. Obviously, not in his hotel room. Why didn't he answer? Was he doing exactly the same as she was? Where was he?

I just want my husband back. Is that really too much to ask?

But maybe I don't deserve him after what I've done.

***

Rob

"What can I get you?" Rob asked as they entered the diner.

"A hot chocolate would be great."

"I'll go and get that table over there," she said, pointing to the far end of the diner.

As he waited for the drinks, he started to feel a bit guilty. Would he be sitting there if Claudia was there? Probably not. Possibly, this girl may be able to help find the photographer. So it's totally innocent, whatever Manny may have implied.

"Here you go," he said, placing the hot chocolate on the table.

Sitting down opposite her, he took a sip of his coffee and set his mug down.

He was struck by her dark hair. It was cut quite straight, just touching the top of her shoulders. Her face was roundish, but her high cheek bones seemed to give her a certain style and a remoteness he had not noticed before. Wearing a sleeveless green top, her apparent casual appearance failed to disguise a certain style he found quite captivating.

"So you want to know my long story?" he asked.

"Yes, please," she replied, sounding overly enthusiastic.

"So, prepare to be bored," he said.

Pulling out the photograph from his pocket, he placed it on the table in front of her.

"That's my mum," Rob said proudly.

"Wow," she replied. "She's beautiful."

"Most definitely," Rob replied.

He spoke about losing his dad, his mum needing nursing care, and her dementia worsening. For all his life, his parents had led him to believe their stay in New York had been bad, but just last week, his mum, despite her dementia, had suggested the opposite.

"This single badly faded photograph, which I found hidden in the loft, is the only tangible evidence of their stay in New York," he explained. "That's why I need to find the photographer. There may be other photos, maybe even the negatives."

Apart from the occasional question, Andrea remained silent.

"So that's my long story," he said.

"Oh boy," she responded. "I'm sorry to hear about your dad, that is awful, and your mum's dementia must be really hard for you."

"It is," Rob responded. "Very hard."

"It's quite a mystery, really," she said

"Well, I didn't see it as a mystery, but I guess it is. So can you help me solve it then?" he asked.

"I'm going to try," she replied.

"If you can't get a reply tomorrow, perhaps you could send a letter to the mailbox."

"Yes, I could, but I leave in three days."

"Oh, is that all? Do you have the address of the mailbox?"

"This is the address," he said, pulling out the piece of paper from his pocket and handing it to her.

"Oh, wow, that's a coincidence. Julia used to live up there before moving to Manhattan. And I've been there once, it's a couple of hours by train. I'll speak to her tomorrow. She may have some ideas," she said.

"Thanks, I really appreciate that."

They both looked at each other.

An uneasy silence fell between them.

"So, do you have a boyfriend?" he asked, and he then immediately regretted asking.

Her demeanour suddenly seemed to change. She opened her mouth to speak, but no words came. He noticed an air of vulnerability that he had not seen before. Something was troubling her.

"Sorry, that's a bit personal. I shouldn't have asked."

Her lips were drawn in, and he could see tears forming in her eyes. She threw her arms around herself and bent forward, desperately trying to control her tears. Finally, her resistance broke, and tears came anyway.

Clearly embarrassed, she got up quickly and rushed to the bathroom.

Stunned by her reaction, he watched her go, feeling completely responsible and unable to help. Two women at the next table who had seen Andrea was upset were now glaring at Rob. Feeling awkward, he avoided looking in their direction.

Five minutes passed, five very long and anxious minutes. During this time, Rob wondered what he should do but realised that the best he could do was to wait.

He fiddled with his coffee mug, noticing a hairline crack by the handle for the first time. Then, just as he started to trace its length, the bathroom door opened, and Andrea was walking slowly towards him, seemingly trying to avoid the gaze of other diners.

Sitting down opposite him, she turned her attention back to the condiments on the table. Rob could see she had been crying, her face now blotchy, and her eyes were still puffy. He sensed he should stay quiet. That she needed time.

An elderly couple got up from a table nearby which caught her attention. As they walked slowly together out of the diner, her eyes followed them until they were out of sight.

"Are you okay?" Rob asked softly.

She looked at him, and then her gaze returned to the table condiments.

"I'm so sorry," she started, wiping her eyes with a napkin. "I've really embarrassed myself and probably embarrassed you. You must think I'm crazy, crying like this in public. To be honest, I think I am crazy."

She paused momentarily.

"I know I should just get over it. That's what people seem to do, isn't it? I'm sure that's what my family back home would tell me to do anyway."

She paused again.

"It's just that I've been dumped," she said, trying to make it sound matter-of-fact. "I know I need to move on. But moving on is more difficult than people think," she added. "But you wouldn't know anything about that being married."

"Actually," Rob replied. "I do."

She looked at him curiously.

"Can I ask what happened… with your boyfriend?"

Andrea stared down at the table, an uneasy silence falling between them.

"I'm not really ready to talk about it."

"Of course, no problem. I'm sorry," Rob responded, regretting asking her.

"You said you understood about not moving on?"

"Difference circumstances," Rob replied, relieved that the awkwardness had passed. "But you know I told you about my dad?"

"Yes, he died."

"He was killed," he paused adding, "By the sister of my wife's friend."

"Oh no, that's terrible," she replied.

"The thing is, I have really struggled to deal with it. I have always felt really guilty about it. My friends, even my wife, keep telling me I must get over it. I know I need to, but I just can't."

Andrea was just about to speak, but Rob carried on.

"Last week, I crashed my car. I was fine, but it could have been worse. But I sat in the car afterwards for a long time and…."

Andrea reached out to touch his arm.

"I just broke down. No one knows I cried like a baby. Now, I've told you."

"I'm so sorry," she said.

"I lost my dad over twelve months ago, and I feel like it was just yesterday."

As he spoke, he wiped away a stray tear. "And you say you think you're crazy?

"What do you mean?" she replied.

"I didn't tell you how I ended up in dance class, did I?" he said.

"Actually, I did wonder about that."

"When I arrived in New York, I went to the only address I had of the photographer. But everything had gone. It was just a run-down area, just behind the dance studio. I was trying to find a cab when three youths with a baseball bat threatened to mug me. This was at the back of the dance studio, where Manny just happened to be. He saw them and chased them off. Manny invited me in to recover, and I asked for his help to find out where the photographer had moved to in exchange for acting as a dance partner. It was all quite surreal. It was just crazy how I ended up there in the first place."

"Oh dear," she said. "What a pair we are."

"Yes, indeed," he replied with a smile.

"Anyway, I really should go," she said. "Thanks for telling me about your dad."

As she gathered her bag together. "I've really enjoyed chatting with you," she added.

"I'll make some inquiries in the morning and call you?"

"That's great. This is the number," Rob said as he handed Andrea a napkin with the number written on it.

They walked outside, and both stood uneasily on the sidewalk, unsure how to say goodbye.

"I'm headed this way to the subway," Andrea announced.

"And I think I'm going in a different direction, but I'll get a cab."

“Speak to you tomorrow,” Andrea said as she walked away.

A cab pulled up, and he settled himself in the back seat. His head was spinning. He had surprised himself when he started telling Andrea how he felt after losing his dad and then how he had cried after nearly crashing his own car. He hadn’t told anyone. He had even downplayed it with Claudia. Why was that? Whatever the reason, he now felt guilty that he spoke to a stranger instead of his wife.

Chapter 19

Rob

Wednesday 15th September

He hadn't slept well. He'd tossed and turned most of the night until he fell asleep when daylight finally started to appear. He jumped out of bed when he saw it was almost half-past nine. Although still tired, he was propelled by the knowledge he was a step closer to finding the photographer.

He picked up the phone and called Claudia.

"Hello," she answered.

"Hi, it's me," he said.

"I tried to phone you yesterday," she said with a slight edge to her voice.

"Sorry, I was out most of the day, but I'm getting closer to finding the photographer."

"Really?" she answered. "After over fifty years?"

"I'm trying to be optimistic," he replied.

"Well, that's a first," she replied sarcastically.

Ignoring her comment. "I'll know more later today. You okay?"

"Yes," she answered. "But I need to rush. Let me know how you get on."

"Okay, I'll call you," he replied, but the line had gone dead before he finished.

Two minutes later, the phone rang again. He half expected it was Claudia. Perhaps she had hung up by mistake.

"Hi, Rob. This is Andrea."

Rob gasped audibly.

"Oh... hi," he answered, surprised to hear her voice.

"I've got news for you," she said excitedly. "With the help of my friend, we've got three possible addresses, with one being the most likely."

"How did they get those?"

"Apparently, she did a property search for Grossman within a mile radius of where the mailbox is. Of the three, one is just two blocks away. The other two are closer to another mailbox office, so I think we may have found the right one."

"That's great. Please thank your friend for me."

"Of course."

"Where do I get the train from?" he asked.

"Grand Central, you will need…." She paused. "This is probably a crazy idea, but could I come with you? I know the right trains to catch, and I've been in the area a couple of times. As they say, two heads are better than one."

Rob hesitated.

"Um," he stuttered. "I wasn't expecting that."

"Sorry, I didn't mean to pressure you. I just thought…"

"You've been really helpful already. I just don't want to take advantage."

"You're not. As you know, I like solving mysteries, and this is certainly a mystery. It's exciting," she replied enthusiastically.

"In which case, thank you," he answered.

"I'm in the office at the moment," she said. "But I'll be able to leave by lunchtime, so let's meet at the clock at Grand Central Station. Don't worry, you will see it in the main hall. Say 1.30 pm?"

"See you there," he replied.

***

Entering Grand Central, the view of the main concourse took him by surprise. He already knew it was one of the largest train stations in the world, but the beauty of the architecture transcended even the physical structure of the building.

Walking down the amazing marble staircase, the clock was easy to see. As he approached it, he saw Andrea waving at him. Wearing a white and yellow striped top and jeans, she seemed to stand out from the crowd. Oddly, he felt a strange sense of excitement. She looked nervous. As he got nearer, she tossed her head back, throwing her hair over her shoulder.

Unsure whether to greet her with a quick hug or shake of her hand, he opted for a simple hello. Standing close, he could detect the floral scent of her perfume.

"Thanks for this," he started. "I really appreciate your help."

"Anything to get out of the city," she replied.

Fifteen minutes later, they were seated on the train headed for Connecticut. As the train was busy, they had to sit apart for the duration of the journey, both lost in their own thoughts.

After a short time, the train emerged from the underground network, arriving at Harlem 125th Street. Fascinated by the changing scene, it held his gaze as the train progressed northwards.

What if this is not the right address? What if all three addresses proved to be dead ends?

But no sooner had these thoughts entered his head, he pushed them away. He had come this far. This couldn't be a waste of time. Claudia would never forgive him.

And then there was Andrea. How would he explain her to Claudia?

She would probably wonder why Andrea was helping him. But surely, there was no harm, and something about Andrea was quite intriguing.

Gradually, the rhythm of the train and his lack of sleep came together as he drifted off.

***

A little further down the carriage, Andrea was immersed in one of her mystery novels. A story about trying to find someone who does not know they are wanted. She smiled at the coincidence of the subject.

In four days, she would leave New York to return to San Francisco to start over. Again. She had already packed up most of her clothes, and Jim would, no doubt, arrange for the rest of her stuff to be sent on later.

Andrea had loads of decisions to make. She would leave Jim behind forever. It would be difficult to say goodbye to Rob in some ways. He's been kind and respected her as a human being. What she felt mattered to him. But he was married to Claudia. How she wished she didn't know her name. Did Claudia know how lucky she was to have him?

More immediately, she was still looking forward to solving the mystery of 'find the photographer and the missing photos'.

As the train neared its destination, her sense of excitement and anticipation increased. She walked down the carriage to find him, and together they stepped out onto the platform. Feeling the cool, fresh air lifted her, quite unlike the familiar smell of the city.

"This way," she said. "Follow me."

A solitary cab was waiting as they headed for the taxi rank just outside of the small station. Noticing their approach, the driver indicated for them to jump into the back.

"Hi," he said in a warm, friendly manner. "Where are we off to?"

"Andrea passed the address to the driver."

"Do you know it?"

"Not specifically," he replied. "But I know where it is."

During the journey, they barely spoke. Andrea worried Rob might feel this could all be a waste of time.

"This is it," the cab driver announced. "The cream house, just there," he said, pointing towards the house.

"Isn't it charming?" Andrea said, smiling broadly.

"With the wrap-around porch, it looks like one of those houses out of a movie. The only thing missing is the rocking chair," Rob observed.

Heading for the front door, they walked down a narrow path bordering a small lawn surrounded by flowers. Set back on one side was a large double garage which almost seemed too big for the house.

"I'm nervous," Andrea said as they walked up the five wooden steps to the front door.

"I just hope this is the right place," Rob replied.

As there was no doorbell, Rob knocked twice.

A few seconds passed, and he was just about to knock again when a woman opened the door.

"Yes," she said.

Dressed in a blue flowery dress, with short white wispy hair, her face seemed to reflect some discomfort. She leant over on her walking stick that she was gripping tightly with her right hand.

"Hello, are you Mrs Grossman?"

"Yes, Cynthia Grossman. Who's asking?" she replied tersely.

"I'm Rob, and this is Andrea, a friend of mine. We're really sorry to trouble you, but we're looking for the photographer Elliot Grossman and wondered if this was the right address?"

She looked at them curiously.

"May I ask why?"

"I've got an old photograph and hoping to get the negative for it."

"You could have phoned first," she said, sounding annoyed.

"I'm sorry," he replied. "I've actually been trying for the last couple of days."

"We've been away," she snapped. "Wait here."

Mrs Grossman disappeared back into the house.

"Elliot, someone looking for some negatives… again," they heard her shout.

They waited anxiously.

Hearing movement in the house, they turned to see Elliot walking slowly, using a stick towards the front door.

Ignoring them, he continued past them, slumping down wearily in one of the chairs on the front porch. Despite the relatively warm weather, he wore a thick light grey sweater which seemed to accentuate his pale complexion.

"Mr Grossman?" Rob asked. "My name's Rob, and this is a friend of mine, Andrea."

"What is it you want?" Elliot asked gruffly, barely looking at them.

"You took a photo of my mum quite a long time ago. I just wondered if you kept negatives from back then."

"I've taken thousands of pictures," Elliot growled in response.

Rob took the photo from his pocket and handed it to him.

Staring at the picture, Mr Grossman pursed his lips tightly and started to rub his chin.

Still looking at the picture. "You turn up on my doorstep, wanting negatives from a photo I took years ago. Are you serious?"

"I'm sorry, I…" Rob started.

Glancing towards the front door. "I'm not feeling well. You need to go," he said sharply.

"Oh," Rob replied, surprised by his reaction. "I'm sorry. Shall we call your wife for you?"

"No, I'm quite capable," he barked, getting to his feet.

"Sorry," Rob said, unsure what to do.

"I'm really sorry to trouble you. We'll go," Rob said.

As they both walked down the steps, Elliot called after them.

"Wait," he said and then peered inside the house. "Come back tomorrow, not before ten and not after twelve, but I can't promise anything."

Without waiting for a response, he turned to walk back into the house, closing the door after him.

“Thank you,” Rob replied but was unsure if Elliot actually heard him.

“What was that about?” Andrea asked as they walked down the path towards the road.

“Not sure,” Rob replied. “It seems we’ve got the right address, but he’s not well, that’s for sure.”

“Not well?” she said. “He was odd.”

“That’s a bit harsh,” he replied.

Andrea shrugged her shoulders.

“We might as well head back to New York,” Rob said despondently.

“That’s a four-hour round trip,” she said. “Wouldn’t it make sense to get a cheap hotel and stay up here?”

“I’m not sure, maybe,” he replied, with the feeling that it might not be appropriate.

“It does make sense, Rob.”

“It probably does.”

They walked silently for a while, but Andrea could not restrain herself.

“I’m sorry, but there is something odd going on in that house,” she said. “I’m sure he’s covering up something.”

“That’s ridiculous,” he replied. “He’s clearly not well, and what is there to cover up?”

“Didn’t you notice the way he was with his wife?” she asked.

“What?” Rob replied incredulously.

“He seemed, well, scared of her.”

Rob just shook his head.

"Aren't you wondering what's in that massive garage?" she said. "I tell you he's covering up something."

"I'm not sure," he replied.

"All I'm saying is there's more to this than he's letting on."

Ignoring her comment. "I guess it would make sense to stay over," Rob replied flatly.

"And I wouldn't mind getting something to eat."

"I know somewhere," she replied. "Julia took me there, and there's a small hotel next door."

Hailing a cab, they headed towards the town. Ten minutes later, they arrived at a café overlooking the Quinnipiac river. Despite the cool late afternoon breeze, they sat at one of the outside tables. Rob sat quietly, watching the small boats glide silently up and down the river.

While Andrea had gone to the bathroom, Rob again reflected on the conversation with Elliot. He seemed to be unwell and clearly struggled to walk. But perhaps Andrea was right. Maybe he was hiding something. Elliot seemed to suggest he had the negatives, but why couldn't he just hand them over. Or at least get his wife to fetch them.

Watching Andrea walk back towards the table, something else was now bothering him. He couldn't help wondering if spending so much time with someone he had just met was normal. But he also had to admit he was enjoying her company, perhaps a little too much.

"Why couldn't he just let me have the negatives? He didn't deny having them, did he?" He said as she sat back down.

"Precisely," she said. "And," she continued. "Did you see the size of that garage?"

"You are obsessed with that garage," he replied, smiling. "Perhaps he still does a bit of photography, and that's his studio?"

"He can barely stand up, let alone take photos," she replied.

"Maybe that's where he hides the evidence."

"What evidence?" he stuttered. Laughing, he said. "You do have a vivid imagination."

"You don't know for sure, do you?"

"I think you've been reading too many mystery stories."

"Don't forget, he's been in New York for a long time, and the Mafia was in control for much of that time. I'm not suggesting he was part of the Mafia, but they may have got him to use his photographic skills for forging passports, etc."

Rob burst out laughing.

"Sorry. But that's completely ridiculous."

"How do you know?" she asked.

"Well, I don't, but it's hardly likely."

"No, it's not likely, but you agree it's possible."

"I didn't say that," he said, smiling broadly

"You didn't have to," she replied before starting to giggle uncontrollably.

Invigorated by her giggling and recognising the ridiculous nature of their discussion, he couldn't contain himself any longer and burst out laughing.

As they headed towards the nearby hotel, she chatted freely, telling him about her friendship with Julia. Rob listened, occasionally turning his head to watch the small boats go up and down the river.

Chapter 20

Rob

Wednesday 14th September

Overlooking the river, he stood at the window gazing down from his second-floor room. But his thoughts were elsewhere. The strange conversation with Elliott worried him. It felt like the possibility of getting the negatives was now drifting away. If Elliot had them, surely he would have handed them over. Why do they have to go back? As for Andrea, she remained an enigma to him. Why was she so keen to come? Although he didn't need her to come, she had been helpful, so it was difficult to refuse when she offered.

Checking his watch, he left the room and met Andrea in the hotel bar. As he walked in, he saw her sitting at the bar. Her hair, now loose, made her look different, framing her face beautifully. There was no doubt she was very attractive.

"I think you like red wine?" she said, pointing to the full glass on the bar.

"Ah, I do. How did you know?"

"Just a guess," she replied, smiling.

"For a few minutes, I didn't think you were coming down," she said.

"Sorry, just reflecting on the day."

"So, do you agree he's hiding something?" she asked.

"I can understand why you think that," he said, laughing. "But the mafia idea is a bit farfetched."

"Maybe, but he's hiding something, don't you agree?"

"Maybe," he replied, still smiling.

"Argh… has anyone told you, you can be infuriating?"

"Yes, my wife."

She had been looking directly at him, but her gaze immediately dropped to the glass she was holding in her hands. She seemed a little unsettled.

"In the diner, you asked me about my boyfriend."

"Yes, sorry that was insensitive."

"No, I was being overly sensitive," she spoke, keeping her gaze on her glass. "Is it okay if I tell you now?"

"Of course."

"We met a couple of years ago. I immediately fell in love with him. My accommodation was horrible but not long after, he asked if I would like to move into his apartment with him. I did have my own room but, let's say, that didn't last too long. I thought he really loved me." She sighed deeply, paused, then took a deep breath.

Rob remained silent, listening carefully, watching her reactions.

"This week he told me he was… gay." Her voice cracked a little. "He's even met someone. Can you believe that?"

"Wow, I can understand why you were so upset."

"We had a really bad argument. He walked out and has gone to stay with his friend until I move out of his apartment."

"That's horrible," he replied. "Particularly after two years."

"To be honest, I can't really get anywhere decent in the city to live, particularly on what I earn so… I've decided to go back home."

He was about to ask where home was when she added.

"In San Francisco, I'll stay with my parents until I get myself sorted out."

"What about a job?" he asked.

"No idea yet. I just need to get out of the apartment, get back home, and try to put it all in the past."

She paused momentarily.

"It's funny. I met an old lady the other day who told me to follow my heart but also listen to my head. I'm still not sure what that means… but it was encouraging."

"Maybe you should be a professional sleuth?" he said, teasing her.

"Very funny," she responded, starting to laugh a little.

"You said the old lady told you to follow your heart. In terms of work, what is it you would enjoy doing, apart from being a professional sleuth, of course," he said, smiling.

She looked at him, a wry smile on her face.

"Before I came to New York, I had a twelve-month newspaper internship at one of the West Coast papers. I really enjoyed that, but I always wanted to move to New York, so I left as soon as I completed that."

"Well, I don't know how internships work here in the States, but you could contact them to see if they have any vacancies. It would be a start?"

Andrea stared at him, smiling broadly. "Yes… it... would," she replied, enunciating each word slowly. "Thank you, I'm not sure why I didn't think of that. I think my head's in a bit of a spin."

"So, tomorrow," he said, keen to get back on the subject. "What do you think will happen?"

Andrea hesitated. "I'm not convinced he has the negatives," she answered. "But then why would he suggest we go back tomorrow?"

"I agree, it's a bid odd," Rob replied.

They debated this for the next hour. Andrea remained convinced Elliot was hiding something. Rob was convinced tomorrow would be a waste of time.

"Well, we'll find out tomorrow," Rob announced.

"That's true."

"I guess it's time to get some sleep," he suggested.

"Agreed, and thanks. I really enjoyed our chat."

She put her empty glass on the bar and went to get off the stool. As she put her foot on the floor, she slipped and fell forwards. Rob grabbed hold of her as she fell against him. Stunned, she couldn't move. Their bodies connected. Although she had regained her balance, she seemed to lean into him. He could feel her breath against his face.

He noticed the barman was watching them.

"Are you okay?" he asked as she stepped back to give her more space.

She stood motionless in front of him, her face flushed with embarrassment.

"Andrea?" As he spoke, he noticed she was wiping her tears away from her eyes.

"I'm sorry, the last couple of days has been tough," she replied almost in a whisper.

"I'm probably more tired than I thought. I should go to bed."

"Of course," he responded softly. "I'll see you in the morning."

"Sleep well."

He watched her head towards the lift, wishing he could help her, but he wasn't exactly best equipped to do that. He signalled for the bill and then headed back to his room.

Chapter 21

Rob

Thursday 16th September

Rob woke with a jolt, the sound of a refuse lorry breaking the usual peace of the early morning. As he contemplated getting out of bed, an avalanche of thoughts flooded his mind. The train journey up from Grand Central, the strange encounter with the photographer, and listening to Andrea talk about her boyfriend. But he was starting to feel a sense of panic, fearing this would turn out to be a total waste of time. Was the photographer just messing him about?

He needed to phone Claudia, but he had to sound positive. Otherwise, she would just say, *I told you so.*

Picking up the phone, he dialled the number. As soon as he heard it was ringing, he could feel a knot in his stomach. But then it continued to ring before switching to the answering machine.

"Hi, just me," he announced, trying to sound upbeat. "Sorry to miss you. Hope all is okay. All going well here. There's a reasonable chance I can get hold of the negs later today."

As he said the words, it even seemed to him that he was being overly optimistic.

"Will try to call later."

Although disappointed not to have spoken to Claudia, he couldn't help feeling a little relieved.

Noticing the time, he left the room, heading for the lift. As soon as the lift doors opened on the ground floor, he saw Andrea waiting by the front door. Her hair was now tied back, and she was happily chatting with the concierge. As he headed towards her, she waved and came to meet him.

"Sleep well?" she asked, smiling broadly.

"Actually, yes, until the refuse lorry turned up."

"Garbage truck," she replied.

"Ah, yes, of course," he said.

They headed outside and sat at one of the tables adjoining restaurant, waiting for a cab.

"Can I just say something?" she asked, looking serious.

"Of course. What is it?" he replied.

"I just wanted to say thanks for last night for letting me tell you about Jim."

"You listened to my story," he replied. "At the diner."

"Yes, but what you told me about my internship made good sense. I'm going to phone them later to see if they have any vacancies coming up."

"I'm pleased I could help. What are friends for?"

As soon as the words friends left his lips, he realised he was being presumptuous.

"Friends?" she asked with a smile on her face. "I like that," she continued.

"Yes, friends," he said. "But I also think it's time to head off?" he added hastily.

Outside there were several waiting cabs. The driver of the first one nodded for them to get in.

Fifteen minutes later, they were outside the Grossman's house.

Walking up the path to the front door, Rob's only thought was how Elliot would respond. The light breeze in their faces felt pleasantly warm.

As he knocked on the door, Andrea whispered, "Good luck."

Seconds later. "Ah, you're back," Cynthia said.

"Your husband told us to come back this morning?" Rob responded.

"Oh yes, I do know that," she replied, wearing an odd expression.

"It's not too cold, so why don't we sit outside?"

"Sure, thank you," Rob replied.

"Perhaps you and your friend could take a seat out there. Just leave the rocker for Elliot. Would you like coffee?"

"We're fine," Rob replied. "I know we've already been a nuisance."

"This is not exactly going to be straightforward, so maybe a coffee would be a good idea?" Cynthia replied.

Rob was clearing his throat.

"What do you mean?" Andrea said.

"I think I will leave Elliot to answer that question."

"I'll go and get coffee. Elliot won't be long… ah, here he is."

Walking slowly and carrying three manila envelopes, Elliot headed to his chair. He was clearly anxious.

"Firstly, can I just say sorry for yesterday? There was actually a reason which I will explain, but I just wanted to say it."

"No problem at all," Rob replied.

Rob and Andrea exchanged glances, wondering what was coming.

"Please understand, this is not easy."

The atmosphere felt tense, and Rob was growing increasingly anxious about what would happen next. Perhaps he was going to refuse to release the negatives.

Elliot leant over towards Rob. "Here you go," he said, handing him two of the envelopes.

"There are five old photos in the envelope which may interest you. Please don't open them now. The photos have yellowed with age, but haven't we all? And in the other folder are the negatives for all six photos, including your one."

"Thank you very much. I really appreciate this," Rob replied excitedly. "I have..."

"Wait, there is something else," Elliot said, interrupting him. "Please bear with me."

Rob started to shuffle in his seat nervously while Andrea was leaning forward, taking in the intrigue. Cynthia came bustling through the doorway with the coffee, placing it on a small table between them. Sitting next to Elliot, she reached out to touch his hand.

Elliot was gripping the third envelope in both hands as if he was worried it would be torn away from him by an invisible thief.

He glanced quickly at Cynthia, who wore a worried expression but then smiled at him in a way that sought to reassure him.

"There is something you need to know," he said, swallowing hard. "But you will need to read the letter in this envelope."

Elliot again leant forward and handed him the final envelope.

Struggling to work out what was happening, he took the envelope from Elliot.

The words written on the front of the envelope grabbed his attention.

In the event of my death, I would earnestly ask this letter be not opened but destroyed. This is my wish that I hope it is respected.

Underneath was Elliot's name.

Rob looked across at Elliot.

"Sorry, what has this to do with me?" he asked.

"Open it, please."

"Are you sure?" Rob asked.

"Rob, just open it," Andrea said, who was struggling to control her anticipation.

It had been so well sealed that he had to tear the envelope open. Then, emptying the contents out onto the small table in front of him, a single sheet of paper, neatly folded, fell out onto the floor. As he unfolded it, his stomach started to tense. The handwriting looked familiar.

An uneasy, anxious silence fell between them. Rob glanced at Elliot, who was studying and watching him closely.

"Please read it," Elliot's voice wavering.

My darling son,

If you are reading this letter, I am guessing you found the photo and wanted to learn more about it. I was never comfortable having it on display at home. That's why I had to hide it.

Before I start, I ask you, please do not judge me. That's all I ask of you, my dearest son.

You obviously know your dad, and I lived for a short period in New York. In many respects, it was a wonderful experience. As you may know, Dad was asked to open the New York office for the company he was working for. It was hard work but also very long hours for him. It was a difficult time for us as a married couple. I wasn't allowed to work, so most days, I would spend my time walking around the city. Quite apart from anything else, it got me out of the apartment, which was always a welcome relief. My favourite walk was from Central Park down through all the districts and stopping for a coffee in Washington Square.

But in the end, I got so homesick that I was desperate to get back to England. As soon as I mentioned this to your dad, he quickly agreed, although I could see the disappointment on his face. I could never doubt his love for me.

About two weeks before we left, I remember one particular day that, although sunny, it was bitterly cold. I stopped at a diner for a coffee and to get warm. Across the street, I saw a photographic studio. On impulse, I thought it would be an idea to have a photo of both of us together. I didn't go in, but when I told your dad later in the day, he flatly refused. He thought it was a ridiculous idea, possibly reflecting the strain in our marriage at the time. But for some reason, that really hurt me. The following day, I returned to the studio, but I went in this time.

It was horribly wet, quite unlike the previous day. By the time I got to the studio, I was wet through. When I said to Elliot that I wanted to have my photo taken, he laughed and said, "Looking like that?" I saw Elliot every day for two weeks after that before we left to come back home. He was kind and considerate at a time that I felt, perhaps wrongly and selfishly, I really needed it.

Robert, I never, ever stopped loving your dad. But Elliot made me feel special. At the time, I felt I was in love with him before common sense made me realise this wasn't true. I was married to your father and never regretted being with him, not for one single day. At the same time, I never regretted meeting Elliot. I know that sounds contradictory, but it was how I felt then.

This is terrible, but there was a real chance that your dad and I would divorce. I've always believed that meeting Elliot actually saved my marriage.

Within a few weeks of being back in England, I discovered I was pregnant with you. I knew Elliot was the father. Your dad never knew he was not your father. That was my decision entirely not to tell him. I didn't tell him as I loved him too much to hurt him. But I did phone Elliot to tell him. I believed it would be wrong not to. He immediately offered to help, but I made it clear that I was not expecting or wanting anything from him. He agreed never to seek to interfere in any way. Elliot was reluctant to tell his wife as he felt sure he would lose her if he did.

A couple of days after the phone call, Cynthia phoned me. She was remarkably calm. I don't know how she got my number–I didn't ask. When no one is asking questions I can keep the truth a secret. The problem is, I've never been able to lie when asked a direct question. She asked if I was having an affair with her husband and she asked why I called him. She wasn't daft, she asked if he'd made me pregnant.I told her everything. She said she wasn't going to challenge Elliot–she was going to wait for him to tell her. I found it odd she could challenge a stranger but she couldn't challenge her husband. Bus she knew her marriage best.

I am guessing you have now met Elliot. Please be kind to him, for my sake. Please don't blame him for anything.

At some point, I guess Elliot will tell Cynthia about you. Both Elliot and I have tried very hard not to hurt anyone but I know we have. In writing these words, I know I am causing you pain, and for that, I am so sorry, but I always felt you should know. Robert, please forgive me for not telling you before. There were so many times that I wanted to tell you, but something always seemed to hold me back.

As the saying goes, actions have consequences, and we both have had to live with those consequences. But the one single positive consequence, and one that I would never regret, was having you as a wonderful son.

Robert, my darling son.

I love you so much.

Mum

Rob felt lightheaded. Was this some silly, absurd joke? Was the letter really from his mum?

"Are you okay?" Elliot asked anxiously.

Struggling to take it all in, he said with conviction, "This cannot possibly be true, no way."

Elliot stayed quiet.

"What is it?" Andrea asked with concern.

Ignoring her, Rob started to re-read the letter. Maybe he had misunderstood what the letter had revealed.

"Are you okay?" Andrea repeated, growing ever more worried.

The tension was palpable.

"Sorry," Rob replied.

He hesitated and passed her the letter. "Read this." His voice full of tension.

Rob watched her closely as she read the letter. Suddenly, she gasped audibly, putting her hand to her mouth in shock. She leant over and placed her hand on his arm. Needing reassurance, he put his hand on hers.

"So let me get this right, you are my real father?" Rob uttered quietly, looking directly at Elliot.

He opened his mouth, and the words came slowly, thoughtfully.

"I may be your real father, but I was never your dad. I said to your mum right at the start that I would do anything she wanted, but she made it clear that she didn't want anything from me, nor could I ever be part of your life."

Elliot paused, then added, "When I saw you yesterday, I recognised you immediately. You look so much like your mother."

"Huh?" Rob said, turning to look at Cynthia.

"And you were fine with all this?" he asked.

"I was never fine with this but I couldn't change anything." She paused. "Elliot only told me last night, but I, of course, already knew. In some sense, we actually shared the same secret. I could, of course, have challenged Elliot, but I wanted him to tell me. It's taken him over fifty years to do it, but at least, there are no longer any secrets."

Rob could feel the anger welling up inside.

"So basically, everyone knew about it except me? The one person that should have been told," Rob said angrily. "You have all lied to me my entire life."

"Rob," Andrea whispered. "At least you know now." Trying to calm him.

"Maybe, but if it wasn't for him taking advantage," Rob said, pointing at Elliot. "We wouldn't have the problem."

As the words left his mouth, he realised the ludicrous nature of the accusation. Looking down at the floor, he could only feel hurt. He had been lied to all his life.

Elliot hesitated momentarily. "I know this is all my fault," he started. "And something like this is hard to take in."

"Seriously, hard to take in?" Rob responded angrily.

He felt he wanted to shout and scream, but inside, he was breaking apart. He desperately tried to control his emotions, but the tears welled up.

For a few minutes, no one spoke. Each seemingly valuing the silence in their own way.

"I'm not sure if I will ever be able to fully understand this," Rob said. "But I don't understand how you have this letter. Why didn't mum give it to me instead?"

Elliot cleared his throat. "I'll do my best to explain. About four weeks after your parents left New York, your mum phoned. She told me she was pregnant, that I was beyond doubt the father, but nothing was to change. She felt I had a right to know but no more than that. She was devoted to your dad. She said, at the right time, she would tell you. She would phone me once a year and tell me how you were doing. Otherwise, there would not be any contact. Until I retired, I heard from your mum every year on your birthday. Every year, she said how proud she was of you. She told me she would write a letter for you and wanted me to hold it in case you ever made contact with me. Within a week, the letter arrived. Your mum asked me to not open it, and I never did," he paused. "And you now have it."

"When was the last time she phoned you?" Rob asked.

Elliot hesitated. "After your father died," he replied. "But I knew she was struggling to communicate. She told me she'd still not told you but would try. She said you might find the photo one day, so I suggested she should destroy it. She was angry that I said that and said she would never do that. She originally wanted the secret to die with her but I got the impression she wanted you to find it, which obviously you did."

"I see," Rob said quietly.

Sitting back on his chair, Rob put his head back, closed his eyes, and sighed deeply.

Suddenly, he turned to Andrea, "We're going," he said, almost in a whisper.

Andrea got up and followed him down the front steps.

They heard Elliot calling after them as they headed down the front steps. But they both kept on going. They walked in silence for a few minutes.

Rob saw a cab heading towards them. He stepped out into the road to make sure it stopped.

"I know we're going back to New York." His voice still shaking with emotion. "But I need to get my head around all this. You go back. I'm going to stay," he said tersely.

She was taken aback. "I'm really happy to stay," she said. "If you want to talk, that's fine. If you don't, that's okay as well."

Shaking his head. "Thanks, but I'll be okay."

"Oh," she replied, unsure what else to say.

She stepped closer to hug him goodbye, but as she did so, he stepped sideways towards the cab and opened the door for her. Without a word, she got into the cab.

"I'll be in touch," he said.

Rob turned and headed towards the town. He felt guilty about sending her back to New York, but he knew he needed time to reflect on everything that had just happened.

Chapter 22

Andrea

Thursday 16th September

The train was close to empty, so she chose a seat next to the window. She pulled out her book from her bag, opened it, and stared at the page. Her thoughts were elsewhere.

She knew she was being ridiculous. Rob was upset and needed space. Of course, he did. His life had just been turned upside down. But however hard she tried to rationalise the situation, she was struggling to get over her feelings of rejection. She could have supported him, but he didn't want that.

She looked again at the page of her book, forcing herself to read the words, trying to convince herself she was indeed, being ridiculous. The journey to Grand Central seemed to take longer than usual, but the train actually arrived early.

As soon as she reached the apartment, she picked up the phone and called the newspaper editor in San Francisco. The editor told her he would give it some thought and call her back, but she was not very optimistic.

She went to make coffee, but as she opened the fridge, she remembered she had run out of milk.

She grabbed her jacket and headed out. Deciding to make the walk a little longer, she walked towards Washington Square, one of her favourite spots. As she walked across the square, she reached where she had met Sally. For no reason, Andrea was able to explain, she felt compelled to go and say hello. On the way, she stopped at a small flower kiosk to buy some flowers.

Arriving at the building, she checked the names listed by the front door. The names against apartment three were George and Sally. Establishing that this must be the right apartment, she pushed the buzzer.

"Hello?" came the response from a female voice through the intercom. She didn't recognise the voice as belonging to Sally as it sounded much younger.

"Hi, my name's Andrea. I'm looking for Sally, but I don't want to disturb her if it's not convenient."

"Is it Sally Bachmann you are looking for?" came the response.

"To be honest. I don't know her surname. I only know her as Sally."

"Hang on, I will come down."

A short while later, the door opened. A lady in her fifties was standing before her.

"Did you say your name was Andrea?" the lady asked, her face friendly but serious.

"Yes, that's right," Andrea replied.

"My name is Ann Bachmann. Sally's my Mum."

"Has something happened? Is she okay?" she asked, sensing something was wrong.

"So she knew you?" Ann asked.

"Oh yes, I met her quite recently."

"Two days ago, my dad died," Ann replied. "He'd not been well for some time, but it was still unexpected. I live in Florida, and when I heard, I got a flight and was here just yesterday afternoon. Mum and Dad were devoted to each other, and when I spoke to her on the phone, she seemed remarkably calm. Anyway, when I got here, the ambulance was outside, so I just assumed it was for Dad. But..." She paused, struggling to keep her emotions in check. "It was for Mum," Ann said. "The ambulance, it was for Mum."

"Oh, no," Andrea cried, putting her hands to her face.

"It seems Dad passed away the previous evening, but she didn't call me until yesterday morning. Mrs. Peters, she lives in apartment 4, went to see Mum about an hour before I got here, and when she got no answer, she tried the door. It was unlocked. Mum was lying on the bed. Mrs. Peters thought she was asleep but..."

"I am so sorry," Andrea said gently.

Ann wiped the tears from her eyes.

"Do you know what her doctor said to me?" she asked. "That she died from a broken heart and..."

The words trailed off as she broke down in tears. Moving closer, Andrea put her arm around her.

"Can I ask you something?" Ann asked, struggling to get the words out.

"Of course," Andrea replied.

"How did you meet my mother?"

"Over there." Pointing across to Washington Square. "I'd just broken up with my boyfriend and was sitting on one of the benches. Your mum noticed I was upset and came to talk to me. That's why I have these," she said, holding up the flowers. "To say thank you."

Andrea paused. "Your Mum didn't know me but spoke to me as a friend. I will never forget that."

“May I ask what she said to you?” Ann asked. “If you don’t want to say, that’s okay.”

Taking a deep breath, she said. “She told me to follow my heart.”

Ann nodded and smiled. “Yes, she really believed that. She often reminded me of that.”

“I better go, and again, I’m so sorry,” Andrea said softly.

“Thank you for coming,” Ann said.

As Andrea walked down the street. She said out loud, “Sally, I’m going to do what you told me to do. I’m going to follow my heart.”

Chapter 23

Rob

Thursday 15th September

As the sun started slipping behind the distant horizon, he returned to the riverside restaurant, sitting at a table directly overlooking the Quinnipiac river. His gaze was fixed on the water rushing towards the ocean, but his head was in turmoil.

Feeling totally drained and confused, he desperately wanted to make sense of it all. But he couldn't. He needed time to process it all, and to do that, he needed to be on his own.

He picked up the pack of photos held together by a rubber band and suddenly realised that he had not yet looked at the five photos. Although the images had clearly been badly coloured by the ageing process, they were clear enough to look at.

The top photo was identical to the one he had found in the loft. The next two were very similar. His mum was just seated slightly differently. But the next two fascinated him. One was of his mum seated on a bench. This wasn't a normal portrait picture. She seemed to be laughing uncontrollably. Rob could feel his heart beat faster, enthralled by the image of his mum. On the back, the words *Washington Square*. But it was the last one that caused him to let out an audible gasp. It was an image of a red brick building. *This must be where mum and dad lived,* he thought to himself. He flipped over the photo. He was right. 'Watson Apartment – Top floor' with the address underneath.

Lost in his thoughts, the waitress appeared next to him to take his order.

"You okay?" she asked.

"Yes, yes, just looking at some old photos."

"What of?" she asked.

"My mum," he replied. He picked up the photo taken in Washington Square and showed it to the waitress. "It's really old, so it is badly coloured."

"Wow, she's gorgeous."

"I know," he replied.

"Food?"

"The pasta, please." he replied.

"No problem," she replied cheerily. "By yourself this evening?"

"Yes, my friend has gone back to Manhattan," he replied.

Sitting back, he again looked out across the river, so many thoughts running through his head.

Twenty-four hours ago, he felt really positive. After some searching, he found the photographer, who said he had the negatives. All he had to do was to collect them and then go home.

Instead, his life had been turned upside down. Not only was his marriage a mess, it now seemed his whole life was a mess. What on earth would Claudia think of all this? Was it even possible now to get his marriage back on track?

The man he had grieved over, the man he had loved for so long, wasn't even his father.

But the revelation that hurt the most was that his mother had lied to him his entire life. In fact, they had all been lying to him except the man who had been a dad to him, the man he had buried.

As a child, his mum had often told him that 'actions have consequences'. It was clear why she said it. She knew it to be true.

But when he thought of Elliot, the anger started to rage again inside. Elliot clearly felt he was the victim in all this. He was no victim. He took advantage of a vulnerable woman living thousands of miles away from home. This was all down to him. This was his fault. And he knew what he was going to do about it.

He pushed his plate aside, his food barely touched, and headed to the street to get a cab.

A short time later, he was standing at the roadside gazing at the house. It was late, but as most of the lights were on, he headed down the path towards the front door.

Taking a deep breath, he knocked on the door.

After hearing a shuffling noise behind the door, the lights on the patio went on, and the door opened.

"Oh," Elliot said. "This is a bit late."

"Seriously?" Rob said sharply. "You dropped a bombshell on me today that has wrecked my life, and all you can say is, this is a bit late."

"The letter was from your mum, not me," he replied, angering Rob even more.

"So, you are saying it's my mum's fault, are you?" Elliot stayed silent. "Well, are you?" As he spoke, he could feel his face getting hot.

"No, I'm..."

"It sounds like you are," Rob said interrupting him.

"Stop it, both of you," Cynthia shouted as she approached them.

They both fell silent.

"Elliot, sit down there. Take this blanket."

"Sit down, Rob."

"I don't want to sit down," he responded.

"We can't change anything," she said. "So, sit down, please," she demanded.

"No, we can't," Rob replied as he sat down. "But your husband thinks he's the victim. He's not. He's the one that took advantage of a young woman."

"You're right, Rob," she replied firmly. "Elliot is not the victim." She hesitated momentarily, then added. "I am."

Elliot turned his head slowly to look up at her, his mouth slightly open, clearly shocked by what she had just said.

Watching her closely, Rob noticed the pain in her eyes.

"Please sit down next to me," she said, turning to Rob. He went over and sat down.

"I've known about all this for the last fifty years," she started. "I've struggled every day to not let it affect my life, to not let it affect our marriage."

Rob opened his mouth to speak, but she gestured to him not to. Elliot just stared at her.

Pulling up a blanket around her, she continued.

"We don't have children," she said. "Three times, I got pregnant, but all three were stillbirths. It was devastating for Elliot and for me."

"I'm so sorry," Rob said softly. "I didn't know."

"Why would you?" she said, swallowing hard, tears welling up in her eyes.

"I always blamed Elliot, but I never told him… until now. It's been hard as I always felt it was my punishment, our punishment for Elliot getting your mum pregnant."

The words stunned Rob. Sitting in silence, trying hard to digest Cynthia's words.

"But how did you know about the pregnancy?"

"Purely by chance," she replied. "I rarely went to Elliot's studio but one day, he asked me to be there as he was expecting some new equipment to be delivered but he was going to a wedding photoshoot. The phone rang, and I answered it." She paused momentarily. "It was your mum. I asked her why she was phoning and after some hesitation she told me. For some reason, I wasn't surprised and even though I desperately wanted to, I never told Elliot I knew."

Elliot looked broken. Tears were streaming down his face. As she glanced at him, the pain and loss of the past fifty years engulfed her all at once. Unable to speak, she put her head into her hands, trying to hold back her tears. But they came anyway.

Elliot started to get up, but she brushed him away.

He was the first to break the silence.

Looking directly at Cynthia but talking to Rob, "I love my wife more than anything else in this world." His words broke with emotion. "Yet, I'm the one who has caused her the most pain." He snatched a breath. "And I know, because of my actions, I have done the same to you. I am so, so sorry."

Rob, unsure how to respond, stayed silent. It seemed the anger he felt towards Elliot was not justified. Their lives had been blighted with so much pain and sadness. Elliot made a mistake, a mistake that had affected them all their lives.

A question formed in his head. *What would my mum want me to do?*

"I'm sorry for what I said earlier," Rob said quietly. "It's all been a massive shock. I know it's really late now, so I should probably go," Rob said.

"Rob," Cynthia's voice sounded weak. "Before you go, can I ask you something?"

"Of course."

"Will you stay in touch with us?"

As she spoke, she stretched her arm out to hold Elliot's hand.

Rob hesitated momentarily. "Yes, I would like that."

"I really wished you could have been our son," Elliot said softly.

Rob was taken aback by what Elliot had just said, but he knew how to answer.

"I am your son," Rob replied. "Not sure about calling you dad, though," he said, smiling.

As Rob turned to leave, Cynthia called after him.

"Maybe we will see you again?" she asked.

"It's very possible," he replied.

After hugging them both, he walked to the road. While waiting for a passing cab, he turned and gazed at the house. He arrived angry and upset that his life had been disrupted, but Cynthia was right. Unfortunately, there is more than one victim.

Sitting in the back of the cab headed back to his hotel, he couldn't stop thinking about Claudia and really wished he could have shared all this with her. Perhaps he wouldn't have been threatened with a baseball bat, but he may have never found Elliot. Nor would he have met Andrea. He liked her, they had got on well, and she had been a good friend.

Chapter 24

Rob

Friday 17th September

He woke to the sound of light rain pattering on the window. Propping himself up on his elbow, he checked his watch. He planned to get the 8:30 a.m. train to Grand Central, which meant he had an hour. Desperate to hear Claudia's voice and to tell her about the letter, he picked up the phone. She answered after the first ring.

"Hello?" she said breathlessly.

"Hi, it's me. How are you?"

"Oh, I'm fine but in a hurry. A bit of a problem with the wedding arrangements, so just on my way out with Suzie."

"I've some good news," he insisted.

"Fine, but it will have to wait."

"But I really want to tell you, it won't take long."

"Are you coming back anytime soon?" she asked.

"Yes, on the flight tonight, so maybe at the wedding."

"Huh, maybe. Don't put yourself out," she replied testily. "I need to go."

And the line went dead.

Feeling hurt but also a little angry, he put the phone down as if in slow motion. He only needed a few minutes to explain everything. But Suzie was clearly more important.

He picked up the phone a second time and phoned Andrea.

***

Claudia

While Claudia was on the phone, Suzie had been waiting in the kitchen.

"That sounded harsh?" Suzie said. "I'm guessing that was your hubby?"

"Yes, sorry, he's driving me insane," she replied.

"Is he all right? Are you all right? We've got plenty of time. You could have spoken to him," Suzie replied.

"He's still on this wild goose chase I was telling you about. Apparently, he's got news. Probably just means he's managed to get a few more photos. It's taken him four days. Can you believe that? What a waste of bloody time."

"It's obviously important to him," Suzie said sympathetically.

"Oh, it's important to him, all right. That's the issue. It's all about what's important to him. And that doesn't include me. Frankly, I've had enough," she replied with frustration in her voice.

"Is this to do with losing his dad?"

"Ha, that's all he's focused on. I've told him he needs to sort himself out, but it just seems to be getting worse."

"I'm really sorry."

"So am I," Claudia replied reflectively. "So am I." Keen to change the subject. "More coffee?" she asked.

***

Rob

As he took his seat on the train, a young couple sat opposite him, probably in their twenties. He was wearing a dark, trendy striped suit and a grey tie, and she wore a pink and grey dress. Just as the train pulled out of the station, a book slipped off her lap onto the floor. Rob reached down, picked it up, and handed it to her.

"Thank you," she said in a high-pitched tone. "That's very kind."

Rob nodded in response. The young man was so engrossed in his book that he seemed unaware of what had happened.

A couple of times, Rob noticed she had to shake his arm to get his attention, but he was back to his book within minutes. She went to hold his hand, but he moved it away whenever he had to turn a page over. The girl was clearly getting a little upset, but she seemed content to accept it.

The girl glanced towards Rob, who smiled back.

"Going anywhere nice?" he asked her.

"Oh yes," she replied excitedly. "We are going down to New York to get married."

Rob was aware his mouth must have fallen open and quickly closed it.

"I hope you will be very happy," he replied.

Rob put his head back and closed his eyes. I wonder if this girl was like my mum, simply wanting to be acknowledged, listened to, and loved. Maybe his dad was so busy working and worrying about simply making a living that they lost their way. Maybe that's why she fell for Elliot. He gave her the attention she needed. As these thoughts drifted through his mind, he realised this all applied to him. Perhaps he was so busy mourning the loss of his father that he didn't listen to Claudia. She reached out to help him, but he rejected her.

He happened to follow the young couple as they left the train.

"We're going to be late," the young man told her as he walked ahead.

"Okay, I'm right behind you," she said in reply, struggling to keep up with him in her high heels.

Rob shook his head in disbelief.

As he approached the main concourse, he could hear a violinist playing on the far side. His music resonated around the building despite the hubbub of the hundreds of people rushing to catch their train. Proficient enough to play in front of hundreds in Carnegie Hall or the Royal Albert Hall in London, fate had determined a more modest setting to receive his musical offering.

Since he arrived, the sky had been a perfect blue, but today was different. Although no longer raining, the sky was now a blanket grey with large pillows of cloud, ensuring the sun remained hidden from view.

As he left Grand Central Station, he readily embraced the energy of the city. He was here for a purpose. The words of his mum rang in his head.

"It's a great place," she had told him. *"I used to walk for hours, so fascinating. You should go soon before..."*

He wondered what else she was about to say. But the words were lost.

From what she had said, she had been fascinated by this amazing city. And she clearly wanted him to experience it for himself. It seemed important to her. So for the next few hours, that was precisely what he planned to do.

As he walked up Fifth Avenue towards Central Park, he felt free, even happy. When he first arrived, it all seemed a little overwhelming, surrounded by so many people, taxis continuously honking their horns, and the buildings almost touching the clouds. In some cases, they did.

Walking slowly past St. Patrick's Cathedral, he was astounded by how it appeared so prominent, so superior, yet much smaller than the surrounding buildings. Its sheer style, age, and architecture simply made it stand out from the rest.

Reaching Central Park, he recalled how Andrea had spoken so fondly of the park. He was sure this would be the one place his mum would have come to.

It was like another world. The fast-paced concrete lifestyle of Fifth Avenue was now replaced by a calm ambiance. Sitting on one of the benches in the Mall, he closed his eyes. As he did so, he felt a trace of dampness on his face from the light rain that had begun to fall. But it could not detract from an image forming in his mind. His mum, sitting next to him, sharing the experience with him.

He had one more stop before he met Andrea.

The usual places visited by many thousands of tourists every year, the Empire State Building, Times Square, and even the Statue of Liberty, would be for another day.

He hailed a passing cab, gave the address to the cabbie, and jumped in. Sitting in the back, his sense of anticipation grew. If he could find the apartment building where his parents lived, he would leave New York very happy.

He stared out of the window as the cab sped down Sixth Avenue, also known as Avenue of the Americas. For the very first time, he really started to understand why his mum loved the city. A place that he knew he wanted to come back to, to visit and visit again. On the streets, there is a certain freedom, but it could also be a very lonely place, a place where you could get lost.

As the cab pulled into the street, he suddenly realised he had been on this street before. The day he went to the apartment where Elliot and Cynthia had lived.

"Can you just drop me here on the corner?" he asked the cabbie.

As he got out of the cab, he felt a sense of anticipation. Heading west, he walked down the street slowly, studying each of the houses as he passed until he came to the address on the back of the photograph. It looked almost identical to the house where the Grossmans used to live. It had tall, narrow black framed windows and a cast iron Z-shaped fire escape. But instead of a black front door, it was dark blue with glass panels.

After walking up the front steps, he searched the nameplate for the top-floor apartment. It read Mr J. Miller.

At least the apartment was occupied, he thought. He wondered if they would let him see inside. He knew it was a long shot, but he had come this far, so why not? He didn't have much time as Andrea would be expecting him soon.

He pushed the door buzzer, not really expecting anyone to answer.

"Hello," a female voice said.

Expecting a male voice, he was surprised.

"Um, is Mr Miller home?" he asked.

There was no response.

"Sorry, did you hear me?" he queried.

"Rob?... is that you?" Andrea asked.

"Oh, sorry... I thought… Andrea?" he stuttered in response, suddenly realising he was talking to Andrea.

"Yes, it's me. Come on up."

Hearing the door release, he opened the door. As he walked up the stairs to the apartment, he felt confused but also elated.

Chapter 25

Andrea

Friday 17th September

She woke from a deep sleep, the first decent sleep in nearly a week. Still half-conscious, she searched for the clock and was surprised to see it was nearly eight o'clock. Learning about the nature of Sally's death still felt raw. She had complained to Jim last week that nothing ever happened. The saying, be careful what you wish for, popped into her mind, which made her smile wryly.

She slipped out of bed. As she did so, she felt a growing sense of anxiety. The last few days' events had changed her life, but it wasn't over. She had a strange feeling today would be the real turning point.

Less than an hour later, the phone rang.

"Hello?"

"Hi, it's Rob. How are you?" he asked.

"Oh, hi," she replied, feeling her heart skip a beat.

"How did you get on? Are you okay?"

"I'm fine. Just wondered if we could meet up?" Rob asked. "I can tell you all about it before I leave."

"Leave?"

"I fly home tonight."

"Oh, yes," she replied, her voice reflecting her disappointment. "I forgot you were going home today. Why don't you come to the apartment, and we can walk to a diner nearby."

She hoped he didn't see it as more than a convenient meeting place. But deep down, there were feelings for him that were hard to control.

"Sounds like a plan," he replied. "What's your address?"

After telling him her address, he said, "That's strange. I think that's the same street my parents lived on. I have a photo of the building."

"What's the number?"

"I'll need to check the photo, but I don't think it gave the actual number of the building."

"So, is two o'clock okay?" she asked, trying to keep her voice steady.

"Perfect, see you then."

As she put the phone down, she could feel excitement rush through her but immediately chastised herself. Rob was married, he lived in England, and she would never see him again, so why on earth was she so excited?

She was just about to go and pour herself another coffee when the phone went again.

"Hello?"

She thought it was Rob again for a second, but as soon as she recognised the voice, she could feel her body tense.

"Oh, it's you, Jim. Sorry, I thought it was somebody else," she replied, trying to calm herself.

"I've been trying to reach you for a couple of days," Jim said tentatively. "I know you said you didn't want to hear from me, but we can't finish it like this."

"You finished it, not we," she replied sarcastically.

"Yes, I know," he replied. "I'm sorry."

"But you're right," she said, "There are some things we need to sort out. When can you come round?"

"This afternoon?" he asked.

She thought for a moment, and the sooner they met, the better. But she didn't want Jim to be around when Rob arrived.

"Can you come round at one o'clock?" she asked. "But no later. I don't want any long, deep conversations, and I need to go out after, anyway."

"Okay," he replied, sounding a little disappointed. "I'll be there. See you later."

She put the phone down and went over to the kitchen counter. As she sipped her coffee, she could feel the resentment and hurt within her. Jim had been lying to her for so long. But in a way, she had started to understand why.

***

At one o'clock exactly, there was a knock on the door.

"Hi," Jim said.

"Why did you knock, it's your apartment, and you have a key?"

"I know, but I said I would be staying with my friend until you found somewhere else."

"Yes, you did. Sorry," Andrea replied. "Thank you for that, but to be clear, I really don't want to know anything about your friend."

"I understand," he replied.

"Not sure you do, but let's drop it."

Andrea went over to the counter and sat down.

"Are you still angry with me?" he asked, looking directly at her.

"That's a stupid question. What do you think? I wasted two years of my life with you."

"I'm sorry," he answered. "I really am."

An uneasy silence fell between them. Andrea had folded her arms and was looking down at the counter.

"I know I should have been honest with you, but I couldn't even be honest with myself. Stupidly, I thought it would change, but—"

"Jim, stop. I am not ready to hear anymore, so please, drop it. All I want to say is that you should have told me how you felt. But you didn't," she paused. "And that hurts."

Jim simply nodded.

"So, do you need help finding somewhere else?" he asked.

"I'll pack a bag now if you like," she responded testily.

"I was only wondering if you needed any help."

"Sorry. I overreacted, but you don't need to worry." She paused, wondering briefly if she should tell him. "I'm going back to San Francisco. I've got a job there."

"Oh?" he replied.

"What do you mean, oh?"

"I was hoping we could stay in touch, perhaps meet up occasionally."

"You must be kidding?" she replied angrily. "Even if I stayed here, Jim, I just can't have you in my life. I can't ever see you again. I feel too much resentment."

"Sorry, I didn't mean..." he started.

"That sounded harsh, but you need to understand that right now, I still love you, and it hurts you didn't say anything sooner." She hesitated. "But I will deal with it over time." She paused again. "Have you actually discussed any of this with anyone?"

"No, not yet," Jim replied.

"Well, you should. When we first met, you were fun to be with. But you have changed so much. You need to talk to someone about how you feel. You need to trust someone. You know, someone told me recently that I should follow my heart. I wish that for you."

Jim gazed at her, crushed.

Another silence fell between them.

"I'm actually planning to fly back home on Sunday, but..." she hesitated. "I can't take all my stuff yet."

"There's no immediate rush," he replied.

"No, I need to get back home to sort myself out, but I can't take everything with me.

"Oh, don't worry about that. I'll organise that for you."

"Thank you. That really helps me. I'm sorry," she started. "But I really need to go. I have an appointment that I can't be late for."

"Oh, okay, I was hoping for a chat. I might not be physically attracted to you, but I still like you… love you... if we'd stayed friends, I'd still have you in my life."

"Jim, there's not really anything else to talk about. It is what it is," she replied. "But thanks for arranging for my stuff to be sent on to me. I'll leave the address on the counter, and remember, just do what I've suggested?"

"I will," he said softly as he headed to the door.

Instead of walking with him to the door, she remained where she was.

Reaching the door, he opened it and turned to look at her.

"Bye, Jim." Her voice, cold and steady, belied the pain inside.

He went to hug her, but she backed away.

"Bye, Andrea."

Andrea stood, her eyes fixed on the back of the closed door. She had told herself she was not going to cry. Enough tears had been shed, but they came anyway.

She ambled to the bedroom, lay down on the bed, picked up her pillow, and sobbed. Slowly, her tears stopped flowing. As she slipped off the bed, she wiped any residual tears away.

After pacing up and down the bedroom, she pulled out her new jeans that she had been keeping for something special. She applied some makeup and then grabbed her favourite cream jumper. She debated with herself if her sleeves should be pulled up or let down. Deciding on the former, she declared herself ready for another goodbye. As she walked out of the bedroom, the front door buzzer sounded. It was not even a quarter to two, so it wouldn't be Rob.

"Hello?" she asked.

"Um, is Mr Miller home?" the man asked.

Who on earth is this guy? Doesn't he know Jim is living somewhere else? She thought for a moment… but the voice sounded familiar.

There was no response.

"Sorry, did you hear me?" he queried.

And then suddenly she recognised the voice but she couldn't understand why he was asking for Jim.

"Rob?... is that you?"

There was no response, but before she asked again, he replied.

"Oh," he hesitated for a second. "I thought... Andrea?" he stuttered in response.

She breathed a sigh of relief.

"Yes, it's me. Come on up. It's the top floor."

"Um, sure," he answered hesitantly. "On my way."

Andrea opened the apartment door and waited nervously for him to reach the top of the stairs. Then, hearing his footsteps, she went out and hugged him warmly.

As she held him, she could feel the tension in his body mirroring her own.

"Come in, come in," she said. "But can I ask, why did you ask for Jim?"

"I didn't realise I was," he replied. "This is the address on the back of the photo, the address of the apartment where my parents lived."

"But I gave you my address?" she queried.

"Yes, I had it written down in my pocket. I recalled your apartment was on the same street, but I hadn't checked the actual number," he explained. "It never occurred to me to compare the addresses... sorry for the confusion."

"Oh, I see," she responded.

"I can't get my head around it," he said. "So this is the apartment my parents lived in."

"It certainly seems that way," she added, smiling.

Andrea was watching him closely. She thought she could see tears in his eyes.

"I can't believe it... and now you live here... I'm not sure what to say."

As Rob studied the inside of the apartment, Andrea went over to the water cooler, poured a glass of water, and handed it to him.

"Thanks."

"I think it would look pretty much the same except for the décor, and I doubt if the kitchen counter would be there. There would probably be a table there."

"Seeing this," he said. "Standing here... well, it's something I will never forget." He paused. "This has certainly made my trip."

He walked slowly around the apartment and ended up at the window. "And this is the view my parents had all those years ago."

"You can have a look in the bedrooms if you like?" she said.

"No. No thanks, just looking around this room is perfect," he said. "And when I see my mum, I can tell her about this."

"Listen, are you still happy to go to the nearby diner at the end of the road?"

"Sure, let's do that," he replied excitedly.

Chapter 26

Rob

Friday 16th September

Approaching the corner of 10th Avenue, he recalled when he last went there after visiting the apartment where the Grossmans used to live. The amount of traffic seemed less, with the sound of the cab drivers hitting their car horns seeming to generate the most noise.

Directly in front of the diner was what seemed to be a tour group, its leader telling them all about its famous history.

"Do you like it?" she asked as they entered the diner. "It's really famous, actually. It's been used in quite a few movies," she explained. "And, of course, Mr & Mrs Watson would have probably visited here as well," she added, smiling broadly.

He did not respond immediately. Instead, his eyes followed the shiny counter running the full length of the diner, the bar stools anchored firmly into the floor, trying to imagine what it would have looked like when his parents were drinking their coffee.

"I've been here before," he said suddenly, now studying the menu.

"Really?" she asked curiously. "When?"

"After I went to the apartment Elliot and Cynthia lived in before they left the city," he started. "It's further away down the street than yours, but I walked here afterwards."

"Wow," she replied. "That's amazing. I come here a lot. I wondered if I was here at the same time?"

"I think I may have noticed you," he replied.

He noticed her blush a little as if he had paid her a compliment. He hadn't realised he had.

"Can I help you, folks? You seem to be taking a long time to decide."

"Sorry," Andrea replied.

"Do you want something to eat?" she asked, looking at Rob.

"Actually, a coffee would be fine."

"Just two coffees, please, cream on the side," she asked. "Shall we grab that table in the corner by the window?" Pointing towards the far end of the diner.

"That's fine, you go over, and I'll wait for the coffees," he replied.

He watched her walk over. It occurred to him that buying her coffee was the least he could do, as without her help, he may never have found Elliot.

When the coffee was ready, he took them over to where she was seated. He couldn't help noticing that she kept adjusting the sleeves of her top and checking her hair.

Sitting down opposite her, he felt a tension that didn't seem to exist before, which he was eager to dispel.

"So, how's the mystery solver?" he said jokingly.

She laughed, which instantly helped diffuse the tension.

"I'm fine," she replied. "I'm just dying to know how you got on."

"I went back to see them," he replied, waiting to see her reaction.

"Oh," she replied, clearly surprised.

"I went back to the hotel to get something to eat. And the more I thought about the whole situation, the more I came to a conclusion this was all Elliot's fault. Although it was quite late, I went back last night to see them, to tell him how I felt, that he wasn't the victim here, and I was going to tell him that. I vented my feelings, which was wrong, but it cleared the air. Let's put it this way, we all have a far better understanding of the situation," he explained. "Cynthia even asked for me to stay in touch."

"So, how do you feel about it all now?"

"Not sure, to be honest. I'm really still trying to take it all in."

He glanced out of the window, briefly watching the traffic pass.

"I still have so many unanswered questions," he added. "But seeing them again really helped." Again, he paused. "I just wish there hadn't been so many secrets."

He stopped talking, his gaze returning to the window.

"Secrets cause so much hurt, don't they?" she said, almost in a whisper.

"That's something I've learnt," he replied. "It must have been hard on my Mum, although she wanted it to be kept a secret as she didn't want to hurt my dad… I mean, the man I thought was my dad… maybe she had the best intentions, but I'm not sure it turned out that way."

"A little bit like Jim, I guess," she replied.

"In a way, yes," he replied. "I don't know him, but I do think he wanted to protect you. Instead, he hurt you, but I really don't think he intended that. He was probably just naïve. Have you spoken to him again?"

She looked down at her hands. "I told him I never wanted to see him again, even as a friend. Do you think that was unfair?"

"I think that's up to you to decide," Rob replied softly.

"So, will you?" she asked.

"Will I what?"

"Stay in touch with them?"

"I'm not sure yet, but probably. Whether I like it or not, he's my real father. They don't have children, and I know he would have liked to have been a proper father to me, but my mum didn't want it. So he really didn't get the chance. That wasn't his fault. And Cynthia was caught up in this mess. So maybe."

A silence briefly fell between them.

"So you're off home tonight," she said.

"I'll be glad to get home," he paused. "After a rather interesting week," he said teasingly.

"Did I tell you?" he said, trying not to laugh. "I went to this dance class a few days ago. I was, of course, terrific, but I had to dance with this girl. Well, she didn't have a clue."

He barely finished speaking before they both burst out laughing.

"I enjoyed our dancing," Andrea simply replied.

"So did I. So what are your plans now?" he asked.

"My plans?" she asked. "What do you mean?"

"You mentioned going back to San Francisco?"

"Oh… yes," she replied excitedly. "I almost forgot… I did what you suggested."

He looked at her, wondering what she would tell him.

"I phoned the Editor yesterday… and he called me this morning and offered me a job," she said gleefully.

"Initially just a temporary role to get me settled in but then a permanent job as a researcher, basically finding and investigating stories."

"It sounds like a perfect job for you."

"Well, I've always been an inquisitive type of person, as you already know," she giggled.

"Like finding dead bodies?"

"Very funny."

"Does the job description include checking out garages?"

"Oh, so funny," she replied, laughing. "You're never going to let that go, are you?"

"Actually, no," he said, trying not to laugh.

She was about to speak but hesitated for a moment.

"I maybe shouldn't say this. In fact, I shouldn't, but…" she hesitated. "I will always remember this week," her gaze fixed on him.

"You are an amazing person," he said, looking directly into her eyes. "Perhaps," he paused momentarily. "Maybe we would have been close friends in a different place and time."

On hearing his words, she slowly dropped her head, briefly closing her eyes as she did so.

His words continued to hang in the air between them, resonating silently in their minds. "On that note, I should probably go," he said, breaking the silence. "I need to get to the airport."

In silence, they got up from the table. As they did so, Rob noticed she wiped her eyes quickly. Following her out, the flowery fragrance of her perfume rose in his nostrils. Breathing in deeply, he savoured the moment. He was sure her perfume, should he smell it again, would trigger memories of the week he spent in New York. As they reached the sidewalk, he sensed an awkwardness with her that was not there earlier.

Standing together, she said, forcing a smile, "I've no regrets."

"Neither do I," he replied.

"If you ever come to San Francisco, let me know. I would love to show you around. This is my phone number," she said, watching his reaction as she handed him a napkin with her cell number on it.

Rob moved closer to her and wrapped his arms around her. As he held her, he could feel the tension in her body mirroring his own.

"Take care, and good luck," he whispered in her ear. "Go and find those bodies."

He turned and walked away.

As she watched him, the emotion of the past few days overcame her. Unable to hold back her tears any longer, she rushed away out of sight. After a few steps, he turned around one last time to wave goodbye, but she had gone.

Chapter 27

Rob

Friday 16th September

After a frustrating five-hour delay to his flight, the plane finally lifted into the sky. As it started to bank to one side, Rob gazed out of the window as Manhattan slowly came into view and, with it, the past few days' events. They seemed to jostle for position in his mind, all demanding his attention. One by one, he managed to push them away. But there were some he could not move.

The anxiety on Elliot's face as he handed him the envelope. The envelope with a secret that has existed for over half a century. A secret that not only changed his life but also changed who he was.

And Andrea's face, reflected hurt but now hopeful for a happier future. A girl in a job she hated, living a life that offered her little. But now following her heart after taking back control of her life. Rob smiled at the thought of her checking out garages.

As for his mum, a guilty secret burdened by her for so long now finally, albeit painfully, revealed. Sharing his own experiences of New York with her, and perhaps, on a good day, she could share her own.

But it was Claudia who dominated his thoughts. She seemed to have avoided him for most of the week. Perhaps she no longer wanted him in her life. And it would be his fault. Such negative thoughts scared him. Any optimism was now displaced by a fear of losing her.

Settling back in his seat, all he could feel was a deep ache that pervaded his whole body.

The emotion of the moment, the realisation of how badly he had treated Claudia, and the revelation about his mother's affair were now consuming him. He felt powerless. Fighting back the tears, he closed his eyes, oblivious to those around him. Whatever anyone thought of him was nothing to the guilt and confusion he was feeling inside. Nothing could ever be the same again.

He remained motionless in his seat with his eyes closed but then felt an overwhelming feeling of exhaustion. Wanting to escape his discomfort, he sought the sanctuary of sleep. Within minutes, he fell into a deep sleep that lasted the duration of the flight.

Chapter 28

Claudia

Saturday 17th September

Claudia first met Suzie at a promotional event for the magazine. They hit it off straight away. With her long blond hair and her piercing blue eyes, Claudia suggested Suzie could do a photo shoot for the magazine. It was an amazing success and they had remained the best of friends ever since.

"How long before we go?" Suzie asked.

"The wedding car is here," Claudia replied. "But I think we have about twenty minutes before we head off."

"Well, I think we should have another glass of bubbles before we go," Suzie suggested.

"Is this where I'm supposed to say to be sensible?"

"Well, you can try," Suzie replied, smiling broadly.

"In which case, I'm in."

"Cheers," Suzie said. "And thanks for being an amazing friend and bridesmaid."

"My pleasure. You look amazing," Claudia declared. "Your new hubby will be bowled over."

"I certainly hope so," she replied.

"Is Rob coming?"

"I'm hoping so. It'll depend on when his flight gets in."

"Oh," Suzie said, starting to giggle. "I need to tell you something."

"What is it?"

"Matt says he is going to ask you for a dance."

"What? Your brother? I hope you're joking. I just can't."

"Of course, you can. He's a great dancer. Just follow him," Suzie replied. "By following him, I mean on the dance floor. Don't follow him anywhere else," she said, teasing her.

Suzie had often said her younger brother was terribly handsome, but the problem was he knew it. He stood out from the crowd at over six feet, with thick rugged hair and lightly tanned skin.

"I doubt he will be asking me to follow him anywhere else."

"Well, he does think you're gorgeous, and of course, he's right. You are," Suzie said.

"I'm ten years older than he is," Claudia replied.

"Mmm… perhaps he likes the mature, experienced lover," she said, giggling again.

"If you didn't have that dress on," she replied, trying not to laugh. "I would throw this champagne over your head."

"Time to go. Time to get married," someone shouted from downstairs.

***

Walking down the aisle in front of Suzie, she sneakily looked across the congregation to see if she could see Rob.

Maybe he'll be here soon.

During the service, she heard the main church doors open and close.

Maybe…

The service finally ended, and the wedding party left the church. As they did so, she again looked for his face amongst the congregation. But he wasn't there.

Sitting in the back of the car, her feelings switched between hurt and disappointment, and she wondered if she was actually wasting her time. Maybe he had no intention of coming.

By the time she got to the wedding reception, her hurt had turned to anger. She felt humiliated. Even if Rob came back now, how could she be sure it wouldn't happen again. She had put her life on hold for him. But maybe not anymore.

Chapter 29

Rob

Saturday 17th September

Unlike JFK airport, the line of cabs was short at Heathrow. In fact, it was non-existent, which was unfortunate as the queue of passengers waiting was long. There was no way he was going to make the wedding ceremony now.

Finally, he reached the front of the queue, with a taxi pulling up shortly after. It was relatively new, almost clinically clean, with the smell of new leather filling the taxi. Checking his watch, it was pointless even going to the church. Instead, he decided to go home. Despite it being a Saturday, the traffic was light, so the journey wasn't as long as he expected.

"Been anywhere nice?" the driver asked.

"New York," Rob replied.

"Never been. Was it business or pleasure?"

"My father lives near there."

As the words fell out of his mouth, he felt he was betraying the man he had loved and admired all his life. But it was still the truth. But saying it made it even more real.

"Anything planned for the rest of the day?"

"Not really. Just going home," Rob replied.

As he entered the house, so many things reminded him of Claudia. A pair of shoes, left at the bottom of the stairs, a scarf tied to a coat hook, and her umbrella lying on the floor behind the front door. Strangely, it no longer felt like home, and he couldn't understand why. Maybe he no longer belonged.

There was now only one thing he really needed to do. To tell his mum, he had her letter and her photograph.

***

The now familiar, distinctive smell of the nursing home welcomed him. Acknowledging a number of the other residents, he made his way to his mum's room, growing increasingly anxious.

As he opened the door to her room, he heard a voice. A voice he had not expected to hear.

"Mary," he said with surprise in his voice.

"Hi," she replied. "Shocked?"

"Not shocked, just surprised."

"Just trying to do my bit," she said, smiling.

"Mum dozed off a few minutes ago," she explained. "She was quite good when I got here but later forgot my name. How was New York?"

"Interesting," he said. "I was thinking perhaps we could meet early next week, and we can catch up?"

"Yes," she replied without hesitation. "I would like that."

"Listen, why don't you get off. I'll sit with Mum now."

"Are you sure?" she answered.

"I'll call you about next week."

As she walked towards the door, she suddenly turned and, to his surprise, kissed him on the cheek.

"See you soon," she said as she closed the door behind her.

Sitting in the chair, he waited anxiously for her to wake up. On the table, he placed two freshly printed photos that his hotel had managed to get printed for him from the negatives Elliot had given to him.

He didn't have to wait long.

"Mum?" he said as she started to stir. "It's me," he said softly. "Rob."

She turned her head to look at him.

"Who?" she asked.

"Rob, your son," he repeated.

"Oh," she replied dismissively.

After a pause, he announced.

"I've been to New York." But his words didn't seem to have reached her. "Mum, I got your letter," he stated, desperately trying to get a response.

Unable to get any reaction, he grew increasingly frustrated.

"I've met Elliot."

Hoping that might trigger a response.

Suddenly, there was a knock on the door. Brenda, his mum's primary carer, walked in with some tea.

"Hi, Rob," she said, smiling. "Your mum has been asking for you this week. She's obviously missed you."

"I've been away," he replied.

Brenda put the tea down and left. Slowly, his Mum turned her head to look at him.

"Mum, are you okay?" he asked.

She seemed to be struggling to find the words.

"Did you find the photo?" she asked, each word taking time to be spoken.

"Yes, Mum, I found the photograph," he replied excitedly.

He placed the new reprint of the photo she had hidden in the attic in her hand. She gazed at the photo as if she was lost in time, and then he noticed the tears forming in her eyes. One by one, they flowed slowly down her cheeks.

"Mum?" he asked gently. "I loved it there." He said it slowly. "I've been there, Mum. I've been to New York, went to Central Park, and walked past St Patrick's Cathedral. I even went to see where you used to live. And I went to a diner that wasn't too far away."

She turned to look at him again. Her face now glowing, her eyes alive.

"The… the… Empire Diner," she muttered, her eyes still fixed on the photo.

"Oh my god, yes, Mum, yes," he replied, so excited by her response.

"You remembered, that's wonderful."

Seeing the tears on her face, he wiped them gently with a tissue.

A silence descended.

"Mum, do you regret it?" he asked.

Her gaze remained fixed on the photo, so she assumed she had not heard. He decided to leave that for another day when she didn't answer.

Slowly, she lowered the photo down on her lap and turned to look at him. Her voice was so clear, he barely recognised her voice.

"We all make mistakes, Rob. It's how we try to fix them that matters," she said. "That's what your dad always said."

"Yes, he did, Mum. He said it often."

"I've made many mistakes," she said, turning to look up at him. "But you were never one of them. You were always special."

Rob swallowed hard, unsure how to respond.

Hesitating briefly, "I've met Elliot."

But her eyes were closed. She had fallen asleep, still clutching the photo.

A few minutes passed, but as she seemed to be in a deeper sleep, he slipped quietly out of the room.

Sitting in his car, he couldn't help feeling unsettled. His mum seemed content knowing her secret was finally known, but she also still felt the guilt that she had carried with her every day for over fifty years. But at least she managed to save her marriage, but he doubted he could save his own.

There was no point in going to the wedding now. The ceremony would be well and truly over. And as he had not made it there, Rob felt sure Claudia would not want to see him.

The last year had been hard for him, but he now realised it had also been hard for Claudia. Trying to relieve himself of the tension in his body, he breathed deeply, but it was a waste of time. Steering the car towards the main road, there was now only one place for him to go.

Chapter 30

Rob

Saturday 17th September

As he walked towards the edge of the cliff, he embraced the cooling breeze on his face. Always fascinated by the sea, he loved watching the waves as they rose and fell, trying to lose themselves in the grey sea's never-ending rhythm. He felt the tension in his body ease slightly, and for a few brief seconds, the guilt and confusion that had brought him to this place seemed to lessen a little.

And then, from somewhere in the distance, a dog barked, immediately pulling him back to reality and forcing him to relive the pain and anguish of the past few weeks.

Despite pulling up the collar of his jacket, his body shivered in the cool Autumn breeze coming off the sea. Although standing perilously close to the edge of the cliff, he eased himself forward to look down. Rob could see someone wearing a yellow jacket, possibly a woman, walking close to the shoreline. The dog ran ahead, chasing the gulls on the beach and towards the next bay.

Closing his eyes, he absorbed the coolness of the breeze on his face, willing it to drive away the thoughts that filled his mind. But however hard he tried, the tension within didn't abate. Unconsciously he licked his lips, a salty taste immediately filling his mouth.

His discoveries over the past week had turned his life upside down. In despair, he tried hard to contemplate his future, but any thoughts stubbornly eluded him.

With the reddening sun sliding slowly behind the sea, he was oblivious to the darkening sky that had started to creep silently over him.

And then, out of nowhere, a moment of clarity. There was something he could do that was within his control.

He stepped closer to the cliff edge and looked down to the beach far below. It would only take one more step forward, and all would be resolved. He was drawn to the moving waves now crashing onto the pebbly beach. Faster and stronger in the rising wind, with splashes of white foam bursting into the air.

He looked straight down to the large rocks lining the base of the cliff, soon to be engulfed by the waves. Surely if anyone fell on them, they would be killed instantly? And what of the body? Would it ever be found?

Pushing these unwanted thoughts out of his mind, he took one of the photos from his pocket. She looked so happy, so beautiful. It brought a gentle smile to his face.

Closing his eyes, he raised his head, looking up at the darkening sky. Despite the wind's coldness and the waves crashing below him, a strange sense of relief and calm now overcame him. Panic and despair were now gone.

He knew what he needed to do.

And he needed to do it now.

Chapter 31

Rob

Saturday 17th September

As he drove away from the cliff, he felt a fresh resolve. He had messed up his marriage. There was no doubt about that, but he was determined to rebuild it. And this was his last opportunity to do so.

He had missed the wedding ceremony, but the reception would still be going on. He was sure of that. But the closer he got to the venue, the more nervous he became. As he pulled into the hotel car park, he could hear the sound of an Abba song, Waterloo coming from the function room. He smiled at the sheer irony of the lyrics.

As the song came to an end, he opened the door to the room. There were several large circular tables with about ten guests to a table and one long table for the wedding party at the far end. To the side was a large dance floor with about twenty or so guests now about to return to their tables.

Still staying partially hidden, he spotted Claudia talking to a couple that she clearly seemed to know. He had no idea who they were.

His initial enthusiasm was starting to wane now. Perhaps this was not such a good idea after all. He had started to walk away when the music started up again. Hearing it stopped him in his tracks. He could hardly believe it. It was the same Elvis Presley song that had been played repeatedly while he was learning to dance.

He turned around and walked back slowly. He looked over to where Claudia had been sitting. To his dismay, he saw a tall, slim guy with thick rugged hair went over to Claudia. Seconds later, she was walking with him towards the dance floor.

Feeling totally thrown, he wondered whether he should just leave. But if he did, he might lose her forever.

It was going to be now or never.

He made his way between the tables to reach the dance floor. As Claudia was looking away from him, she was not able to see him approaching. Swallowing hard, he ventured onto the dance floor.

With a confidence that seemed to appear from nowhere and feeling like he was in a movie scene, he tapped Claudia's partner on the shoulder. The guy turned to look at Rob.

"I'm her husband," he announced. "Do you mind if I dance with my wife?"

Clearly surprised by Rob's request. "Of course," he responded, immediately walking away.

Claudia stared at him. Her face expressionless. If she was surprised to see him, he couldn't tell.

He gazed at her. She looked as if she may have been crying, but he wasn't sure. Wearing a dusty pink dress with a lace trim that hugged her body, she looked incredible.

"Shall we?" he asked, holding his arms out in his rehearsed dance hold.

Avoiding eye contact, she stepped forward, taking her position. The familiar rose scent of her fragrance made him want to pull her close, but he resisted.

In other circumstances, they would probably have fallen apart with laughter. But there was no laughter, just genuine anticipation.

He tentatively took the first step, eager to place his feet in the right position. No words were spoken. No words were needed, not yet. Although there were some misplaced steps, his confidence grew slowly.

As they moved with the rhythm of the music, their bodies slowly came closer together until they were moving as one. Rob could feel every breath she took, every move she made, but he could also feel a hesitancy, a tension within her.

As the music ended, they stood apart, unsure of what to do next.

"We need to talk," she said quietly. "But not here."

There was a hardness in her voice that worried him.

"Where?" he enquired, noticing she was avoiding eye contact.

She hesitated before responding. "I planned to stay here overnight, so why don't we meet in my room?"

"I can take you home. My car's here."

"No," she replied abruptly. "Here."

He nodded.

"I need to give my excuses to Suzie. So meet me in my room, 121, in ten minutes."

"Okay," he replied. He reached forward for Claudia's hand to lead her off the dance floor. But as he did so, she turned away and returned to her table. Although relieved the dance routine was okay (he was sure Manny would be pleased), he felt a terrible weight in his stomach. She seemed to want to talk, but the thought crossed his mind that perhaps it may now be too late.

As his mouth felt dry, he stopped off at the hotel bar. He considered a brandy to help him calm his nerves but eventually settled on water before heading to room 121.

Standing outside her hotel room, he took a deep breath before he knocked. A few seconds later, the door opened. He walked in, closing the door behind him.

"Before you say anything, I need to ask you a question," she said, staring at him.

"Absolutely," he replied, feeling his stomach tense even more.

"You lost your dad twelve months ago," she paused momentarily. "But at the same time, I felt I lost my husband." Then, pausing again, she added. "Have I lost you?"

Her question seemed to hang in the air between them.

"After what I put you through," he replied. "I actually thought I had lost you."

"Because you blocked me out," she replied. "You wouldn't let me in. I'm your wife, for heaven's sake."

"I'm sorry. I know you're right. But sometimes, you wouldn't listen to me."

"What do you mean?" she asked.

"Last weekend, when Jeff and Maggie came around," he started. "I asked you not to invite them, but you did. Not only did they come to our home, but you invited them to my birthday dinner. And you wondered why I was so upset and angry."

"I guess we're both at fault." Her voice was softer. "But you hurt me when you shot off to New York. You didn't for one minute think about me." She paused. "I had visions of you disappearing off into the sunset with a young American girl. I was hurt…"

Rob was taken aback. He had never mentioned Andrea, not that he would go off with her.

"Anyway, I've given up my job working for Jeff, so I won't invite either of them around for dinner anymore."

"Thank you," he said simply. "I need to tell you about New York, I did try on the phone, but you were too busy."

"Actually, I wasn't too busy. I was just angry with you, with myself. Sorry," Claudia replied as she went over to sit on the edge of the bed.

"What I discovered in New York has been a shock, but it also made me realise one thing. That I love you more than anything. I wish now you could have been with me."

Claudia looked down at the floor and stayed silent.

"I know I've messed up," he started. "I know that, don't ask me why. Really, I don't know, I can't explain it."

He drew a long breath. After a few seconds, he muttered. "Oh my god, I don't want to lose you. I…" he muttered, turning to face the wall.

The words dried up, despite his desperate efforts to compose himself. He felt ashamed, but now, all of a sudden, he felt very alone.

"Rob."

Hearing her voice, he swung round to face her. He saw tears flowing freely down her cheeks, and his heart went to her. Then, without any spoken words or further thought, they moved towards each other as if in slow motion, an almost surreal action.

And then they embraced. There was no hesitation, no reservation. Their needs were so very different. Rob sought her forgiveness, a chance to put things right and move on.

The fear of losing her had been tearing him apart. He was angry with himself for being so selfish, and then slowly, he could feel something inside him giving way, and the tears started to flow.

As they held each other, he caught a glimpse of her in a mirror on the wall next to them. She was looking at his reflection, and their gaze met. Somehow, their reflected images did not seem real. He looked into her eyes and saw the hurt he had caused, but then quite eerily, he started to see something else.

Something of greater significance. He saw, for the very first time, his future, even his destiny. This was the woman he really loved.

Her eyes closed slowly, as did his.

Their needs were being met in the silence that now enveloped them, and the quietness conveyed the knowledge that the days, weeks, or even months ahead would not be easy. The past twelve months could not be easily forgotten, and their love for each other now had to be rebuilt. They needed to start again.

But for now, for this special moment, nothing else really mattered.

Epilogue

Four Weeks Later

After the wedding, Rob took Claudia and Amy to New York. The time for secrets was over. Well, most of them.

They walked through Central Park, gazing at the building where his mum and dad used to live. And then had lunch in the Empire Diner.

The following day, they went to see Elliot and Cynthia. By then, Elliot's health had worsened, but despite that, they spent the day with Elliot and Cynthia reminiscing about life in New York fifty years ago.

When they left, Cynthia walked with them as they headed down the front steps towards the road.

As he hugged her goodbye, she said, "Thanks for coming to see us. This has been really special. Not just for Elliot but also for me." She paused momentarily. "Elliot didn't want me to say anything, but he was told yesterday he only has a few weeks left. He rarely cries…." She swallowed hard, her eyes brimming with her own tears. "But last night, he was inconsolable. Not because he has little time left but because he feels he let you down. I tried to tell him it wasn't his choice, but he felt so guilty. But seeing you and your family today has really made him very happy."

For a moment, he froze, unsure what to say.

Turning to Claudia. "I'll be back in a moment," he said quickly and ran back towards the house. The front door was open, and as he walked in, he saw Elliot sitting in the armchair, looking down at the floor.

He knelt on the floor next to him.

"I just wanted to say thank you," he said. "For caring, maybe loving my mum at a time when she needed someone. Despite her dementia, she still remembers you. I will always love my dad, but I'm so very glad we met."

Unable to speak, Elliot nodded in response, tears in his eyes.

Walking back towards the door, Rob turned around. "Take care," he said, his voice starting to crack. He hesitated briefly and then added, "I love you."

***

Returning to New York on the train, Claudia and Amy chatted eagerly throughout the journey. But Rob spent most of the time gazing out the window, reflecting on the time spent with Elliot and Cynthia.

Arriving back in the city, they walked through Central Station, stopping to listen to music being played by yet another lone aspiring musician. But their final stop was to see Manny. Claudia had been keen to see where Rob had learnt his few dance steps, the dance steps that may have helped save his marriage. Manny could not have been more delighted to see them. After much cajoling, he persuaded Rob to dance a few steps with Claudia under his watchful eye. Amy almost cried when she saw them dancing together.

He wondered if Manny would make any reference to the mugging incident or even his role as a last-minute dance partner. But not a word was spoken of it.

They were exhausted when they boarded the plane to return home. Amy was the first to fall asleep. Then, as Rob and Claudia settled down, she leant over to rest her head on his shoulder.

"Just one question," she asked, whispering in his ear. "Cynthia happened to mention that a friend of yours was with you on your first visit to see them. Who was she?"

Immediately, he felt the tension rise in his body.

"Oh, that was Andrea," he said, trying to make it sound matter-of-fact. But he sensed Claudia was waiting for a fuller explanation.

"I met her at the dance class, and she asked why I was in New York. I told her about trying to find Elliot. It was actually she and a friend of hers that managed to locate the address. As I was not familiar with the area, she offered to travel with me. She was really helpful."

"I see," she replied flatly.

"She lived in the same apartment my parents lived in. I think it was fate that she was there to help me find Elliot," he added. "I didn't mention it earlier as I didn't think it was important."

"Are you in touch with her?" she asked.

"No, of course not. She moved to California."

"Are you able to contact her if you need to?"

Remembering that she had given him her contact details, he hesitated.

"Yes, she gave me her phone number, just in case we visit California, as she would love to show us around."

"I see. Do you have any plans for us to visit?"

"None at all. I see no reason why we would want to do that."

"Okay. Just wondered," she replied.

A silence descended between them. Adjusting the blanket underneath her, she said, "I'm really tired. I think I'll get some sleep."

"You know I love you, right?" he said softly.

"Yes. I do," she replied. "And I love you unconditionally. By the way," she whispered. "You never did tell me how you ended up at Manny's."

"Ah," that's a very long story.

"I suspected it might be," she said. She paused, looking away momentarily. Turning her head back to look at him, she reached for his hand.

"You know I want to write a book and I have some specific ideas, but," She hesitated. "I wondered if you would mind if I wrote about your story?" A short silence fell between them before Rob answered.

"That would be amazing," he responded, gently pulling her closer to him. "I would like that."

Within minutes, they had both fallen asleep.

***

Six Weeks Later

Two weeks after Rob and the family travelled to New York, Cynthia called to say Elliot had passed away. Even though Rob had been expecting it, the shock of losing him still hit him hard. Putting the phone down, he headed toward the kitchen, where he knew Claudia was preparing dinner.

"Who was that?" she asked without turning round.

"Cynthia," he replied, his voice heavy with emotion.

She spun round. Claudia knew from the haunted look in his eyes it was bad news.

"Elliot passed away during the night."

Without any words being spoken, she moved quickly toward

him. Wrapping her arms around him, he held her so tight she could barely breathe. Although no tears were shed, he felt consumed by a deep regret that he had not known Elliot earlier. He knew this man could never replace his dad, the man that had raised him, but the connection with Elliot was real and tangible.

***

12 Months Later

As Rob was driving home along the coast road, a news item on the radio mentioned the heat wave affecting New York. Barely a day went by without some memory coming to the forefront of his mind.

But it was the pain to Claudia that remained his biggest regret. There were times when she would be concentrating on something, and he would gaze at her and remember how he had hurt her so badly.

But they had managed to move on–he had discovered in her someone who had given him a renewed foundation for his life. Ever since the day they embraced in the hotel room, they had embarked on a new journey that had led them to a far closer and more intimate relationship than they had ever experienced before. She had just published her first book, which included a special dedication to Rob's mum and Elliot.

But as he looked out across the sea with the images of New York drifting through his mind, he smiled to himself as he recalled discovering the New York his mum and his Dads would have known. Until then, he had not understood what they must have gone through. He wondered why his mum had never told him about Elliot, but perhaps, she had tried to, but he had not listened. He had so many questions.

But now, most of those questions had gone. Rob knew his mum loved him, and he didn't need to know anything else.

As he approached his home, he saw in front of him his life, a life that had been changed forever. As he turned off the road towards the house, he whispered, “I’m home.”

The page had been turned.

The End

Milton Keynes UK
Ingram Content Group UK Ltd.
UKHW010647140923
428660UK00003B/88